KARACHI TO MALABAR

An Odyssey of Love

SANJEEV PANACKAL THOMAS

INDIA • SINGAPORE • MALAYSIA

Copyright © Sanjeev Panackal Thomas 2023
All Rights Reserved.

ISBN
Hardcase: 979-8-89133-861-6
Paperback: 979-8-89067-789-1

This book has been published with all efforts taken to make the material error-free after the consent of the author. However, the author and the publisher do not assume and hereby disclaim any liability to any party for any loss, damage, or disruption caused by errors or omissions, whether such errors or omissions result from negligence, accident, or any other cause.

While every effort has been made to avoid any mistake or omission, this publication is being sold on the condition and understanding that neither the author nor the publishers or printers would be liable in any manner to any person by reason of any mistake or omission in this publication or for any action taken or omitted to be taken or advice rendered or accepted on the basis of this work. For any defect in printing or binding the publishers will be liable only to replace the defective copy by another copy of this work then available.

An Odyssey of Love
My gratitude to AEM, the painter, and a Disclaimer

Anjolie Ela Menon is my super senior in school, whom I had the opportunity to see from a distance as she visited Lovedale in the early 1970s. She was lively; she had a disarming smile on her face, and I still remember her walking past with childlike enthusiasm to the happy onlookers, so proud of her achievement as a painter. I understood none of it until ages later when I was old enough to appreciate art.

Those moments are still etched in me. I have drawn inspiration from her paintings to depict my characters in the manuscript of my novel, which has a tinge of Lovedale, where we both basked in the sun and fog.

DEDICATED TO

My twin brother
who still lives entwined in me and whom I discovered through this odyssey

Appachan
My grandfather, who deluged me with love

Asha
My sister, who went without saying goodbye because she could not see me cry

EPIGRAPH

"A million people's breath was snuffed away as they waited to inhale the air of freedom."

Michael
Chief Protagonist

Contents

Foreword *11*
Prologue *21*

1. Xariah................................... 25
2. Eliza's Twins 38
3. Nirvana 44
4. Train to Karachi........................ 49
5. Mannanda Angelic 54
6. Zohal, the Moon of His 65
7. Smile Enigmatic........................74
8. The Departure 84
9. Amsterdam Calling 91
10. The Swearing-in....................... 96
11. My Life, My Love 100
12. Love Child............................ 105
13. Birth on Wings 116

14. The Thunderbolt... 123
15. Mystical Malabar... 128
16. Forgotten Lives... 134
17. Prodigal Son... 140
18. The Lass... 149
19. Arrest Without Warrant... 153
20. The Suicide Pact... 160
21. Zohal & Eliza... 167
22. Eliza, Flashback... 175
23. Michael, the Rising Star... 183
24. Till Death Do Us All Part... 199

Epilogue... *207*
About the Author... *209*

Foreword

KTM #anodysseyoflove, as I would like to call it, has been churning in me for a long time. I am more of an athlete of reasonable repute with a school fan following of quite a few than a person with the creative bent of a writer. I am more of a natural athlete.

But I have been enamoured by those who could write—the gifted writer who could put words in your wandering mind to express it in all its lucid bareness. You see it sprouting in your own visualisation; it is being made into enthralling music and dance forms; it is being screened in front of you as a movie. You feel light, you feel happy, you smile at yourself, you even smile at a stranger, and the smile becomes contagious, thanks to the writer, like the natural swimmer who takes to water like a duck, or the natural writer whose pen pens down, eyes closed, enthralling literary creations.

I too wanted to be among those who could spread that smile that's so contagious that it may one day be as contagious as the Coronavirus, with the difference that people could just not have enough of it.

It was difficult.

You can speak a thousand words, but try writing a hundred. You sit staring at the spiral-bound book, twirling the pen between your fingers in search of a creative urge, or gaze at the laptop screen in confidence at an AI-enabled wonder. Gibberish is all you get.

Then the moment of reckoning arrived. It was exhilarating. Do or die. I decided to take the plunge, with my eagle hands spread wide, gliding in the wind, eyes wide open, ready to enjoy the thud to the ground, for that would be my first, and I wanted to relish the last moment of it.

To my utter surprise, after the initial fall, I rose; my hands had taken wings; my nose had peaked; and my body had feathered. My hands penned what my mind spoke; it was synchronous; it was as melodious as the sound of an awakening flower, awaiting his messenger of love to carry his inner self to the pining lover and to her womb to flower future flowers of immense beauty.

I became a writer thus.

The pent emotions, joys, angsts, heartbreaks, and hopes I experienced, the experiences I heard from my parents, the events that unfolded in front of me, and the morning dreams that spoke volumes all came alive as I glided the wind to be myself.

Each one of us has a writer, a greater depth inside. Do you want to search and bring it to the fore, or do you want to be your lazy self and let it be lost forever? I chose the former, and that's how KTM was born and took wings.

You would have heard of writer's block, but have you experienced one? I have been privileged by both. The first chapter was written seven years ago; and the next seventeen took seven months. It coincided with the most difficult times of my entrepreneurial journey, where nothing seemed to work and when your most trusted just abandoned. You couldn't, as it's your baby, and I, for one, will never, because that's the reason why you were born!

It was an arduous journey meandering through treacherous waters. I waded slowly but resolutely. The hungry crocodiles were amused and let me pass with a smile. Some patted too, and but that was when I realised that the genuine and brave will never be let down. In that comfort of auto mode, I found time to pen my thoughts and my vivaciousness. Thus was born my KTM #anodysseyoflove, which has all of me in it and a whole lot more of my fantasies.

I have been in two minds about whether to speak of it, for it might be too close to real-life situations than the fantasy that I have portrayed in the book. But I felt it would be unbecoming of me if I didn't state it. It would be a big let down to someone who guided me back to life to be able to write this book..

KTM has a bit of me as a character and a lot of me as angst and hope. I have a tinge of myself in Eliza's twins. My survival was possible only by the visit of an inebriated doctor, who had come to borrow some money from my father for his journey forward. He got it and left, seen off by my father.

There comes the twist of the tale as he returns an hour later with a ticket home, not utilised as the doctor in him sobered him. He felt ashamed that he had abandoned a newborn fighting for his life. He spent the next twenty-four hours tending him and parted, saying he would live.

Well, that was a celestial appearance, as neither my father nor I could not locate him since then, to the best of our efforts. My twin was lost before the celestial intervention. I was told that my twin looked destined to live as he was healthier, and he showed it by kicking and crying while I was listless. In the deepest of my unspoken words, I was telling him to conserve his energy, like a hibernating polar bear.

He did not listen, preferring to play to the gallery with his whims. Deep in slumber, I did not know of his departure until I was five years old.

Then I realised he had left his soul with me to don it for life. I have done it; he's my alter ego, and he has been the inspiration for this book. I knew he would be vastly different from me, but for the looks, He cherished life and love at their epitome. The character Salim was born out of it. To me, that's the soul of my book.

The characters Avira, Michael, Eliza, and Devon all have a tinge of the stories I have heard in my sane life. I have nourished it with my fantasies, and I bear it before you in all humility.

That's the story of KTM #anodysseyoflove.

❋ ❋ ❋

FAMILY TREE

Varghese Mappilai - The wealth builder

Jacob and Avira - The brothers

Eliza and Sarah - Daughters of Avira

Mannanda and Varkey - Panackal family heads

Cherian, Paulose, and Michael the children

Sosha, Mariam, and Eliza, the daughters-in-law

Devon, Salim, Mohan, Ayesha - Michael and Eliza's children

Daisy - Mohan's girlfriend

Pallavi - Daisy's daughter

Colonel Azmaray - Pashtun Family Patriarch

Zohal - The daughter

Tamzin - Zohal's daughter

Andam Durrani - Tamzin's husband

Xariah - Tamzin's daughter

Amar - Xariah's son

OTHER'S in order of appearance,
1. Neelakandan and Savithri; Panackal Doyens
2. Daizee, the paramour
3. Imran, Station master
4. Mathen Dy Chief Minister, Daisy's father
5. Sivadas, young legislator
6. Jacob Pothan - Daisy's husband
7. Professor David - Salim's guide
8. Dr. Ayaan - Medical intern and Xariah's friend
9. Abhijit Banerjee - Mohan's batch mate at JNU
10. Iqbal - Family driver
11. Ariyan - Caretaker, Malabar
12. Jaanu - Ariyan's wife
13. Govindan - House boy
14. Paaru - Chief Maid
15. Lolita - Paaru's daughter
16. Cheman - The local blacksmith
17. Thiruthi - Cheman's wife
18. Saroja - Cheman's daughter
19. Anthony - Devon's best friend
20. Chacko - the neighbor
21. Sebastian - Sub Inspector of police
22. Cherumi - The enchantress

The rest of the characters and the events referred to are etched in history, and a web search by the reader will bring forth the roles and events referred to. For the e-pub version, I have provided a web link that will take you to those events. I have chosen the websites carefully so that the information you get is not clouded. Further, I have provided a link to my email for answers to native words, characters, and events.

I would recommend base reading or research into the myth of the formation of Kerala, the land mass rising from the seas, lord Parasuram wielding his axe, Iringol Kaavu, the mystic and famed temple that dates its origins to the Mahabharata; and Yakshi, the enchantress the celestial nymph of local fables of Kerala. Interestingly, she resides atop the palm tree, waiting to seduce and devour handsome males from the land. A must and engrossing read would be the deeply ingrained caste system in Kerala of the early 1900s. This would make the reading of the book deeply involved.

Being a story spanning three generations from India before independence to the 21st century, do brush up on the history of the land we learned. While the events and characters bear true, the sequence and timelines may have been altered for the sake of storytelling.

Prologue

The long, flowing robes of his were not very different from the rest of the merchants.

The ship had just anchored at Krangannore, one of the most prominent trading ports for spices in India then, nestling the sea on one side and caressing the backwaters on the other. As he descended to the shore, people could not escape the gait and gaze of the lanky man, who sure was not a merchant, for his body gave it away. He had the build of a man who toiled for his daily bread and a countenance that radiated wisdom. The world would realise centuries later how the spread of Christianity outside Jerusalem began.

Apostle Thomas was received with open hands by the king of Krangannore, who was a scholar in arts and religion himself. Declaring that Hinduism is the cauldron where all thoughts blend and evolve, he allowed Thomas to preach his gospel. The young head of Panackal Illam, Neelakandan Namboothiri, was enamoured by the concept of religion and worship that Thomas brought forth. It had just one theme. Love; keep loving; love even when someone despises you. Love even if someone hurts you because the only truth in the world is love.

Neelakandan, almost the same age as Thomas and his wife Savithri, were the first to embrace Christianity outside Israel. For Neelakandan and Savithri, it was always a journey of love and ecstasy blended into one. People would say Savithri had divine power in her dance. An apsara in reincarnation. Each morning as the moon set, Neelakandan and Savithri would merge in a conjugal dance, with Savithri raising herself like the fanged cobra dancing to the ecstasy of her beloved. That was Apsara's rebirth.

Daisy could not believe her eyes as Pallavi rose from the array of dancers around her, performing her version of Vaasuki the snake guardian. The gods and rakshas had used Vaasuki to squeeze out the Amrit, churning the seas, the ambrosia of eternal life, found by the Rakshas, to be stolen by the gods, Vaasuki in witness. Pallavi rose her hood in full spread, devouring the Amrit and serving justice to the whole world.

It was a spectacle.

The heads of nations witnessing the special event to commemorate the Nagasaki holocaust were the first to rise in reverberating applause.

Chapter 1

Xariah

Salim walked into the pub early in the afternoon and moved towards his favourite seat at the edge of the counter, from where he could see all, but he masked away from the view of others, akin to adorning the invisible cloak of Harry Potter.

Bell in Tavern was his favourite. Loved equally by the well-heeled and the students, it had the eighteenth-century charm blended in with youthful quirkiness. The singers and the comedians had an equal degree of fan following. The college students made a fast buck working at the pub. It enabled them an occasional one-night stand, pleasing the soul and filling their wallet.

Though tempted, he desisted as Salim was working on his doctoral project. His thesis was that the humans were devilishly honest after the threshold of intoxication and that they seek out their souls with no inhibition. In the course of his observations, he witnessed many transitions that made a meek an overbearing with a propensity to express their sexual desires even to a total stranger, once intoxicated to the hilt. Although it taunted him, he stayed away from it because he wanted his thesis to be unbiased.

It was the last Friday of the month, and it was ritualistic for him to adorn his native attire. Salim prodded in with his grandpa's umbrella as a companion. He was dressed in the native attire of Mundu and Veshti, the skirt-bottomed trousers that had no cleave and the round-necked shirt that buttoned sideways. All in a pastel hue. He had a gold-laced long scarf thrown over his shoulder, serpentine and winding down. The wedding headgear of the Chaldean faith perched on his head like a crown, it could be parsed a style statement or an expression of deep angst. Those who saw him for the first time were amused. What the heck is he wearing?" Few could understand its symbolism and even less people the depth of what it represented.

The grandfather fables had taught him the history of Christianity in India and the attire he was wearing a remnant of it. Christianity had found roots in Travancore much before it became a fad and the faith in Europe. In Europe, it grew into an institution of unparalleled power and authority that the royals swore to protect with their own lives. No king could ever think of being crowned in a ceremony other than at the Sophia, with the tower of Babel in witness. It was a reminder as to 'what can happen if the king displeases the God or his anointed one on earth, the Pope'.

Salim's grandfather Appachan was well-read. He would say, "While the poor had to live as a good samaritan all his life for a place in heaven, the rich could make a hell out of a heaven on earth and still get a ticket to heaven through the 'direct to heaven' certificates. They they could buy it" from the Pope, with their money well or ill gotten.

Salim thought, what if I chanced on one?

"Well, there must be some finer screening at the entrance to paradise for the most blessed to be seated next to the apostles. It may be a password to be remembered or a sign only known to the three. The heaven certificate had the insignia and signature of the pope, hence just the password".

Salim prayed that the password be simple, in case he chanced to have the certificate.

Jesus was a meteor.

Three years is all he has had since his re-appearance to spread his message of love and inclusion. He shook the very foundations of religious beliefs until then. Paul, the biggest contributor to the transition and growth of the preachings of Jesus into a religion, was a disbeliever to start with. In fact Paul was most trident critic of Jesus. . The Lord would say,

It took my celestial appearance on my resurrection to transcend and make him a believer"

And what a believer he turned out to be, his trusted, the erudite and most talented.

For a breed of sun worshippers in Europe, the gospel of love that touched their soul was an ambrosia to salvation. Peter spread the faith with his master oratory and his unparalleled organising adeptness. He started a movement that took the form of religion that gave the millions in Europe a reason to live life meaningfully, knowing that their deeds would one day be rewarded in an afterlife in heaven. It gave them a reason to look beyond violence and conquest. It fascinated all and stirred a movement that would make it the most-followed faith in the world.

But it took not too long for the discerning to understand that what spread in Europe was Pauline Christianity, the material and power-oriented religion, rather than the love-thy movement that Jesus founded. The Pope not only went on to be the emperor of emperors but also regressed scientific thought through repression, brutal coercion, and control in the name of religion. Michael Serviettes, whose discovery would save millions later, was burned at the stake. He was a physician. Galileo, who spoke the true words of the creator, showing the world what the universe really looked like, he was jailed for life.

The church had turned evil.

Even the fallen angel Lucifer, lowered his head in shame at what it had become.

The birth of Christianity in India was vastly different. The doubting Thomas was assigned by his master to spread his message of love in Asia. The land of spices, Kerala, was his first destination. He travelled with wealthy merchants who traded pepper from Kerala, the black gold, and other exquisite spices that formed the gourmet lifeline of Europe. St. Thomas and his message of love were welcomed with open arms at the palace gates of the king of Krangannore. Through his debates on religious beliefs and the essence of Jesus's thoughts, he won over an influential section of society, with many discerned inspired to take to the new faith. "The essence of life is knowledge. I welcome new thoughts, and anyone who wants to embrace them is welcome to do that". Those were the words of the Krangannore ruler.

The scholar class of Namboodiri's were enamoured by the concept of un-conditional love that Jesus brought Forth. They were to be the first to embrace Christianity outside the Jewish land. As a descendant of Panackal Illam, the first family to embrace Christianity in India, Salim prided himself on his ancestry. He had wowed to be the torchbearer of a dwindling lot, but an epic remanence of history. He had promised his grandfather, "Wherever on earth, I will adorn the attire that represents my family roots and ethos once a month"

He never broke that promise.

"Here is your nectar, Salim."

For a change, let me offer you the latest, a dark pilsner'. The voice was not familiar but it was inviting. He looked up at the sight of a girl of medium build with a smile that resonated.

"I know everyone who works here, so who's she?"

Sensing the predicament and wanting to end his misery, she patted his shoulder tenderly. "I am Xariah and have been on duty for a month now. I have been watching you and your queer ways since then. Well, I thought it would be fun to surprise you."

Yes, she did more than surprise him. The petite lady had the distinct features of a person from the mountains. The green eyes, the sharp nose, and the texture of her all pointed to that. But there was something more that gave her far more elegance, as though an enigma. Salim was intrigued and couldn't resist asking,

"Xariah, sweetheart, what's your story?"

Xariah's father was with the embassy of Pakistan. Andam Durrani was from an affluent Pashtun clan with lineage to the tribal chief. He had chosen to be in America as the fluidity of politics back home troubled him. He had decided that it would be best for his family, especially for his daughter, to be out of the country so that she could pursue her passion. Her father was sacrificing his senior bureaucratic privileges back home to put a big smile on her face.

"This is for you, my child."

Andam would embrace his daughter with the deepest of warmth and say,

Xariah's mother, Tamzin, was an adorable Twitter. She had black eyes, unlike Xariah or her grandmother. Her eyes sparkled in merriment. Her smile encapsulated her, and the eyes spoke more than her words, as though a heart-to-heart conversation started the moment the eyes locked. Xariah, like her mother, was the only child of her parents.

"No word of your grandparents?"

He quizzed Xariah.

"Oh, Ama"

she replied.

"She refuses to leave her heavenly abode in the mountains. Seldom has she done that since Grandpa went missing. She still longs for him and waits for him. But we have a whale of a time when we meet'."

"Went missing?"

Salim could not make sense of her words. It must have been in the war; how traumatic for the young lady then. He did not want to hurt her feelings. He knew going missing on the battlefield would be so scarring. The wait never ends, as he could still be alive. "Ama still has the fleeting morning dream that Grandpa is back. I know she misses him a lot."

Xariah finished her story.

Over the next few weeks, they would meet and converse at length on subjects ranging from her field of study to music and movies. They were yet to date, but Salim had become fond of Xariah. He now longed for her presence.

Am I falling for her?"

Xariah was unlike the other women in his life so far. They were hedonistic and alluring in that sense. There were a few serious relationships that did not last the test of time and numerous one nightstands that faded before dawn. His love was his thesis now. But with Xariah, he had a metamorphosed draw on her. She was astute, distinct, and brutally honest. Besides, she was an attractive mountain filly too. Soon, they were dating.

Each encounter drew them closer.

Xariah's birthday was approaching, and Salim wanted to surprise her with a special gift. The surprise gift—the unknown side of him to most He would cook for her the rhapsodies of Travancore cuisine, *pidi and irachi,* the rice ball and brown beef curry that Mannanda, his grandmother, had taught him to cook.

"Boys need to learn cooking; after all, Nala, the Hindu god of cuisine, was the best chef ever."

She would quip.

Cavernous inside, it was her way of securing that her grandchildren revered women. Having grown up in a patriarchal family, she had seen men as the recipients of all good things in life, from affection to all necessities needed.

"What a spoiled lot."

She would lament. They would have the preferences when meals were served, leaving a soiled platter for the girls to wash. They would grab the Sari hem, the long drape that women wore, to dry their hands, then wipe their faces with it. Salim would notice the exceptional stiffness that some of them had as they took the wipe, as though it were an erotic act.

"It seemed to mask their sexual inadequacy."

Mannanda, too, would feel the repulse, and she was determined to set transformative standards for her children. She declared

"The boys will cook, the girls will wash dishes, and all will wipe their faces on a towel."

Xariah was amused at his cooking. Taking it for granted, she teased Salim.

"Baby, shall I sharpen the knife and help you slice the meat? Maybe I do the recipe and you wash the dishes. Let's not waste the venison; it's precious and expensive.

Salim enjoyed the tease; it had a shimmer of yearning. Swooning, Salim humped her and perched her on the sofa on the balcony. She sank into the softness of the clouds. It was so comfortable that he knew that Xariah would not budge from its comfort for long.

"Your favourite jazz and some Barolo red to go with it to relish your meal, dear?"

She gave a dove-eyed look that meant yes.

In the luxury of comfort, she was too lazy to even nod. She loved the food. Resting her head against his shoulder, savouring the wine from the same glass, she whispered in his ear, biting,

"I want to devour you, my lover boy!"

Chapter 2

Eliza's Twins

Salim and Mohan were clones.

Eliza had delivered twins prematurely, and with the rare condition of their inability to self-feed, the newborns looked destined to die.

It was not whether, but when.

Stories were galore of their elder siblings, who would take a break from their boisterous outings to peek and poke to see if there was any sign of life in the strange forms that looked more like an overgrown embryo than a newborn.

Eliza's father, Avira, was a pious man and a strong believer in destiny, having lost his second child before she turned a teenager. She was plucked away by the calm waters of the stream interlacing his paddy fields as she walked to deliver lunch for her father, tagging her elder sister Eliza.

Sarah was different, very unlike Eliza or anyone in the family. She was the epitome of joy and a chirping firefly who saw the world in its true beauty. No qualms, no regrets, no expectations. She just loved to be free. She would hug her dad every day and put him to sleep with her little lullabies, and for Avira, who had lost his mother early in life, it was a strange but joyous remembrance of his mother.

The day Sarah died, the whole world seemed to have paused a moment, as if in a rare attempt to rewind the clock by a few milliseconds to save the little angel. He cursed everyone for the misfortune.

He grudged Eliza as she was to be her angel protector. Why did she walk ahead of Sarah? Why did she not carry her on her wings rather than make her walk? Why did she not sense her queer slip into the waters as she searched for glowfish in the pristine waters of the stream that meandered through their rice fields?

For Avira, It was the work of Satan who schemed against Jehovah, and his daughter was caught in the crossfire. It devastated him, but he was unwilling to blame God. God had bigger plans for her, Avira convinced himself.

Awakening from his thoughts of Sarah,

Avira made his decision: his grandchildren are to live or die as Christians. He declared there would be an immediate home baptism. In the Jacobite church that dates back its history to the days of St. Thomas, a home baptism was difficult to digest for some of the parishioners, and that too at such short notice. Avira, being the Kaikaran, or the laity representative of the church, who had made an immense contribution to it, stood firm, and the church had no option but to oblige.

He then said, "Thou, I thank you. They are safe in your hands. I swear in the name of Jesus the healer that I will second-baptise my children at Parimala, the abode of the holy saint who spread the teachings of Christ far and wide in

Travancore. They will be offered a slave to him, my lord."

It was a masterstroke. What choice did God have other than to grant the wish of a believing grandfather? Be branded as heartless-soulless who left to stay on the sidelines, letting events take their course, destroying the very foundation of faith. The assembly of gods unanimously declared

They are willed to live!

The survival story of Eliza's Irattakal, the twins had the whole town in ecstatic joy. Second baptised, hail and hearty, Eliza beamed at each baby step her twins took. She looked with overwhelming pride at her precious jewels, destined to go places. Her trusted astrologer had professed to her,

"Oh mother, your moolam nakshatra star-borns are invincible together; they will rule over people one day."

But how would slavehood evolve? they wondered. The twins were relieved when they heard from their grandfather that the slavehood was until the day of their marriage.

"You have to go to Parimala, pray in gratitude, and break the penance of slavery, seeking his approval for the wedlock."

Wryly, he said, "Sons, you can't be slaves to two at a time; hence, before you marry, you will be set free, the freedom till your nuptial tie, to be held in bondage forever." He was laying to rest any misconception the twins had that they can ever be unshackled of slave-hood.

Salim was enthralled by the concept of an eternal slave to the saint. Only in fables had he heard of such relationships between a willing slave and a benevolent slave master.

A naughty slave and an ever-benevolent slave master—that's what it turned out to be. Salim could never be confined to one; he was an eternal lover. He saw himself second only to Krishna, the blue-bodied deity who preached Dharma to Arjuna at war and stole the robes of bathing damsels with a mischievous smile, with the same ease.

"That's the truth of the lifeline on my palm."

He would muse. Krishna had made concept of life simple for him. The tattoo on Salim's back stretched serpentine, Krishna, and a thousand damsel-gopikas in an enchanting embrace.

It radiated tantric-sensuousness.

"Don't I look like Krishna on my tattoo, from an obtuse angle?"

He would laugh out loud at his grandfather.

Chapter 3

Nirvana

Salim had returned to India on a sabbatical in preparation for his new book.

When in search of inspiration, it's always been the nature-caressing hamlet with dove-eyed lasses that spurred his creative best.

Salim bid farewell to the dark-hued Daizee.

It was the first time he had ever said goodbye to someone, as he believed those he met were destined to meet again in a life long friendship.. It was strange, as his favourite theme had always been:

> 'Never say goodbye, as we are destined to meet again."

As he walked back to the beach, the hapless plea and lustful tear in her eyes, as she parted pierced him, hitting him like the waves growing rough, lashing against the rocks and splintering into droplets the size of tear. What was she conveying?

"Please don't say we will never meet again."

Or, was it a plea?

"Kiss me and take me back for one night more."

Maybe it was a cry to be con-joint slaves drinking and devouring each other. Salim was unsure if he had done it right.

Her tears haunted him. He longed to know her inner soul. Back at the beach, Salim closed his eyes, transfixing to the moment Daizee walked in. Emerging from the faded walkway to the subtle hue of illuminance, she looked unfathomable in her inner desire. Transfixed, her eyes teased him and lusted for him like Rethi, the goddess of erotism.

"Am I dreaming?"

Then it struck him like lightning; "Weren't these the eyes that teased me in my intimate dreams? He had searched everywhere during his trips north to south to meet the lady with the vampire eyes, the one in his innermost dreams and desires. He had given up all hope. Now in a serene hamlet that merges with the lake, there she was!"

"Nothing short of a miracle"

Salim reminisced.

When he received photographs of three girls to choose from for the night, it was the same old story of selection: 'slim, white, and beautiful. Donned in fashionable clothes that did reveal the cleaves, they looked like triplets. A man who believed in concept of equality, he could not decide.

"How can I ever discriminate based on gender, colour, or craft." the thought

It was the very foundation of his thought leadership program. He wished the lady had included a lust column too while she sent the photographs.

"All three or none."

He told her, More is disgust over the choices than the novel attempt of a foursome. And that's

when the portrait of Daizee flashed on his screen.
"The dark-skinned Daizee" he replied,

"It's Dusky Daizee and she chooses the price!"

The moaning seemed eternal.

Kissing passionately, he thrust into her. Reaching the crescent as he exploded, Daizee bit him deep in the ecstasy of the moment. It really hurt him. She had never experienced anything like it before. Her husband had impregnated her and left. Her married lover returned to his lady. She hadn't been aroused for ages since then. And now, it all came back, riding on a thousand horses. She found in Salim her suave, dirty lover. The pang of her womanhood un-shackled, their body and mind convulsed in a mating tango of the cobra. As he lay fatigued, just beginning her ascent, Daisy tore into Salim like a hungry predator. Only in his wettest of dreams had he experienced anything close to it.

He opened his eyes and longed to see her beside him, to inhale her. The heaviness of expectation for the next rendezvous weighed heavily on Salim.

'The Adonis edifice could fall'
He cautioned himself.

"Goodbye, Dusky; we will not meet and mate again. The Shiva-Parvati Thandavam, the bliss of mating, has happened between us. It's once in a lifetime that the fangs of Shiva bite deep with such ecstasy. Let those moments be etched for life."

Let me tell you, Daizee, that our coming together was so close to my eternal hug with my twin brother, his crotch resting against my cheek as we lay embedded in our mother's womb. It was the only moment that surpassed my deep dive into you.

"Is this not called Nirvana?"

✳ ✳ ✳

Chapter 4

Train to Karachi

Chettathy, Mariam had not slept the whole night. Her firstborn Rajan, aptly named the King, had kept her awake through the day with his tantrums.

Michael was on a journey to unite his sister-in-law, Mariam, with her husband, his elder brother Paulose, who was a JCO with the British army, posted in Karachi.

As the train chugged into Hyderabad Sind in the morning wee hours, they had an opportunity to buy milk for Rajan. It was the lack of it that caused his pestering. Grabbing a quarter, Michael walked in search of milk, and there it was: Rahil's fresh and hot milk, which seemed to have been open in the morning hours only for

Rajan. Michael yearned for a hot cup of spiced tea, a specialty of Karachi, but a quarter would just be enough for Rajan's milk. Michael had it tempered the way Rajan would drink; a few drops on his palm savoured it; he knew it was perfectly blended. She could cuddle her son into his sleep now, thanks to Kochupapi, as he was fondly called.

Mariam had always wondered if Mike was not her firstborn. After two years, she was going to see her husband. As she cuddled Rajan, their first meeting flashed in front of her. Mariam found Paul transcended even on their first meeting. Paul's father had come seeking her hand for his son. She remembered that Paul did not smile, but his eyes were kind. The deepest of her fears was whether he would live long enough to return her love. She knew the vagaries of being a soldier with the British. Paulose longed to be a teacher, but circumstances had him fighting for the British, whom he despised for colonising his motherland.

He was a celebrated soldier and an instant celebrity back home in the remote village of Methala. All in the village longed for a suitor like him. Mariam and Paulose got married during his earliest leave available from the army. He was not a passionate lover. He seemed much older than his age in his expressions. Mariam, just sixteen, longed for him. But she understood soon that the burden of family weighing on her husband, the torchbearer of an agrarian family that had his father a sublime role, would be away on duty most of the year.

A week after the wedding, Paul had to leave for the barracks. Mariam gave him her soul as he went back to the war. Michael was a year older than her. He was intelligent, a reader of literature, and a boy with incredible leadership skills. He could convince anyone with a sound argument. He was handsome, with looks that no girl could take her gaze away from. To Mariam, he was her firstborn. Michael, too, placed her on the pedestal next only to his mother. He could feel a rare comfort in being with her. Michael would bury his head in Mariam's lap when he felt lost. What a dichotomy—a younger woman giving the solace of a mother.

It was a bond nurtured for life.

As he turned around, with milk in his hands, he heard the whistle and chugging away of his train to its ultimate destination, Karachi. He was startled, but soon became calm as he realised there was no way he could catch the train or stop it gathering the momentum as it went. He drank the warm milk to the last drop, one that was bought for his nephew. It was the best decision then; the milk tasted so good.

He knew Chettathy would realise what had happened and would trust him to be by her side when she wanted him the most. As the train arrived, there was a team ready to receive Mariam. Michael arrived a few hours later. He had met the station master, Imran, and narrated his story. The rest just happened. Imran was amused and fascinated by the youngster who left his sister-in-law all to herself in a foreign land but had immense confidence that she would be fine. He was put on the next train to Karachi with mes-sage going to the station master of Karachi of the incident.

Mariam was diminutive.

Her mother-in-law Mannanda, eclipsed her in beauty and gait, but the inner composure with which she caressed and controlled her army husband was the backbone of the family that kept it together. The rare occasion on which Michael showed his emotion was when Chettathy passed away. He sobbed like a child. Even when his father died, he did not feel the pain so much.

Chettathy was the black hole that took everything coming its way, cleansing the giver.

Chapter 5

Mannanda Angelic

Paulose's quarters were nestled in the quiet corner of the cantonment in Karachi.

Being the storekeeper in charge and a gentleman soldier to the core, he held a position of authority far above his rank that many of his peers and seniors envied. When his family arrived, the quarters became a bustling get-together spot for families in the cantonment. The weekends were splashed with home-cooked food and gin and tonic to spice it up. For Michael, it was the meeting and melting pot of all his age in the neighbourhood.

Michael and Paulose were very different, but for the blood that flowed in their veins. Paulose had taken after his father, who was serious, hardworking, and had a dark skin tone like him. Michael was like his mother, Mannanda, handsome and pale, who could be mistaken for a Pashtun.

It was Mannanda's second marriage.

At the age of eleven, she was a widow. She did not even know what that meant. The only change that it brought to her life was that she now moved back to be with her parents. Ironically, that was the most joyous moment of her life.

Varkey had quietly admired Mannanda as a young boy but could never gather the courage to express his feelings towards her. Not only was she the most beautiful girl in the land, but she was also from an elite family that would shun a reach out for alliance with his family.

As he learned of Mannanda's marriage to the wealthy suitor, he was sad and took a vow of celibacy. As if the gods were hurt, the wealthy suitor did not even get an opportunity to hold her in a caress. He died young.

And Mannanda did not cry.

She did not even know this guy, who was made her suitor in a ceremony called a marriage pact between the two families. She was never even explained as to what it was, let alone be asked for her will. The only thing she remembered were the giggles of the servants and the respect that she suddenly commandeered among the family elders. It looked surreal, and it haunted her.

The pall of gloom in the house lasted a while. The chirping bird that she was became quiet. She could not attend school, as the norms for widows forbid it. Confined to homeschooling, she would sit gazing at the fields as girls of her age ran to school in a boisterous raillery. So engrossed would she be in the spectacle that she failed to notice Varkey, who would pause each day to catch a glimpse of her in the hope of getting a glance back.

Once Varkey turned sixteen, he gathered the courage to tell his father his wish to marry Mannanda. Mannanda had turned thirteen by then. She was now more beautiful than an angel now, with locks of flowing hair and sharp features that were almost Greek. Her skin tone was paler than the full moon, seeping through the winter sky; she was the epitome of beauty. Mannanda had attained puberty that year, which added a rare glow to her face. The chirpiness came back. Her smile could turn a thousand faces.

She now deeply longed for a lover.

The following fall, they were married. He was hailed as the giver of life to a widow. To him, it was the greatest joy of his life.

"The fairy tale really happened, my princess."

He would tell Mannanda. He looked after her like one. For her, he was the lover boy who would express his deepest emotion for her in the utmost subtle manner. She was amused at him holding back his deep desire for her. She would tease him through the morning wade in the stream that curled the fields and hold him in a serpentine embrace that left him gasping. To her, he was a slave of a lover who just wanted to be bonded, sheathed, and led on like the children of Pied Piper or be the puppy on a leash that wanted to be cared for, caressed, and kissed—one who would return the love to his master, guzzling night and day, in the fondest of fantasies.

As she lay naked in the moonlight, Varkey shed all his inhibitions and made love as if they were born only for that.

Michael was third in line. When he was born, he was as pale as the winter moon, with a rare olive glow. Mannanda took deep pride in her third son, her clone. Taking him in her hands, she raised him for the whole world to see and kissed him on his lips, in a true mother-son moment. She had always wondered why mothers don't kiss their children on the lips to draw them into an embrace of the deepest love that they shared while in the womb. Mannanda would never wither away from an opportunity for the most precious moments like these with her children. She would say,

"The inheritance that my children will have from me is my time. It'spricier than gold, as my life is limited while gold reserves are unlimited".

The thought touched Varkey's heart. He ensured that his wife was never burdened with the chores of the house. Although second in line, Paul was second only to his father, Varkey, in matters of the house.

The eldest son, Cherian, was a rare fusion of his parents. The looks of his father, the bonhomie of his mother, and the utterly carefree attitude of his own He had charted out a path for himself early in life—a wild life that had him wield a hunting gun even before he had reached his teenage years.

Varkey was worried when Cherian used to disappear with his friends for the hunt, with no notice to his parents. After drying the hunt on the behemoth jungle rock, he would march home with the venison, sporting the victory smile of a warrior, days later. Mannanda celebrated her firstborn, who quaffed the spirit of her ecstatic union with her lover husband. She was glad that the unbridled lovemaking through night and day gave her son the spirit of a hippie and a life of immense freedom.

"My boy has achieved his freedom and hippiness at such a tender age." She would gleam.

Mannanda loved him for it.

Cherian loved everyone and never grew beyond his teenage days to be the darling of his nephews and nieces. To the next generation, the lasting enigmatic smile on his face was so inviting and comforting that they knew that the Wild West's fastest off the block, Cheri-Wood, in pun, would be there to protect them from all the evils. The stories of his nieces knee-balling those who dared their friends were folklore.

The kids just could not have enough of Cherian.

When Cherian moved to the jungles in Malabar to start his estate, his ardent fans followed him. They had to wade waist-deep water in the summer to reach his land by the side of the river. The monsoon would be a deluge that needed a ropeway bound to the trees on both sides of the river to cross. Swinging on it, Cherian would ace it faster than a chimp.

Stories abounded;

That he had kneeled the Ottayan or the lone elephant in lust with a mesmerising look. They lapped it up in joy. The folklore had much more. The invite of the lovelorn damsel of the jungle with the darkest skin and the lust of a celestial concubine was turned a dumb ear by Cherian. It was unbelievable, a moment of folklore ecstasy, that made all wonder how he could resist the temptation of the most desirable.

"Was he gay, or was he incapable?"

Bemused, Cherian would preach to his followers, "The universe was created in six days. On the seventh day, God rested. Man too has the power to transcend to the level of the creator in bringing forth a new life". "Six days of passionate lovemaking with your love of life, and the seventh day you rest as the creator did. You will have a progeny as beautiful as your world."

The profoundness was astounding. He was soon to have a co-creator. Sosha was as cherub and carefree as Cherian. Of all the suitors that came her way, she dismissed the wealthy and well-heeled to literally run away with her wayfarer lover suitor. Was it love at all? she wondered. It was the eternal freedom that she saw in a life with Cherian. The instant attraction turned into a burning desire to be with him. It braved her to shed the comforts of her wealthy parents and turn a vagabond, flying into the arms of Cherian, relishing the eternal freedom it gave. Every day until the day she passed away, Cherian would kiss her passionately in the morning. Looking into her eyes, which had a lingering melancholic tinge, he would wonder each morning,

"Was it worth it, my dearest, to be in this rover love lock with me? You could have been the Queen of the Hills had you chosen one of the wealthy suitors."

Did she ever feel it or regret it?

Sosha sensed his guilt. To her, it was the pristine moment of un-shackling; the very moment he took her into his arms, she was liberated.

The wealthy Jacobite Christian family had its own norms for girls. The freedom to be a butterfly and live your soul was never one of them. She could live naked in the precincts of her room. It liberated her. The moment she stepped out of it, it was the 'elegant' dressing that devoured her inner self.

To be free is to be like nature. Nature never hides her innocence and beauty through a sheath."

She would argue with herself and her peers: The trees are so beautiful as they are naked; so is the swan. The peacock dazzles the whole world with his nude rain dance.

"Why robe me? Darling, you made me the richest person on earth".

Sosha murmured to Cherian. They would be in a passionate love lock from then on, every morning, until the day she departed. Those who saw her in the cask could not miss the ecstatic smile on her face, one of having lived full and parted well.

Cherian did not shed a tear.

He knew that would be the biggest disrespect to his wife. He kissed Sosha on the lips to the bewilderment of the grieving folks; it was his parting gift to her. He realised it was as warm and passionate as his first kiss. He would live a full decade more in the warmth of that kiss.

'Sosha's smile had merged with his.'

His great-grandchildren noticed the fusion of the souls, and to them, they had Sosha and Cherian in one.

They even debated among themselves.

"Was it Ammachi Sosha who died or Appachan Cherian?" For no more is Appachan what he was. He had taken wings to flutter around with all smiles. All of Sosha.

They loved the new Avatar of Cherian!

***

Chapter 6

Zohal, the Moon of His

The deep blue eyes of Zohal transfixed Michael at the first sight. He did not know what had hit him; it was a thunderbolt moment. In a moment, he was a forlorn lover, with the only desire left in him to blend with her.

Zohal had walked in with her father.

Colonel Azmaray, who commandeered the rifle companies, oversaw the affairs of the store that Poulose headed. The Colonel had a special regard for Poulose, who was diligent and a gentleman officer to the core.

When the colonel was informed of the Paul family's arrival, he was keen to meet them at their quarters, a rare gesture by a colonel.

As Michael was introduced to him, he had disbelief drawn large on his face, which was difficult not to notice. In his jacket, Mike looked every bit a Pashtun except for his eyes which were black, and the build which was smaller. His charming smile radiated on his pale skin, which turned orange at dusk. Colonel Azmaray extended both his hands to Michael in a warm clasp. He patted his back as though he were one of their own clan as he settled for tea. Michael accepted the greetings with gratitude, all this while his heart and gaze were on Zohal walking alongside her father.

As Zohal was introduced to the family by her father, Michael felt that he had known her for ages. The curiosity of Zohal towards the instantly affable Michael gave way to teenage curiosity.

Is it infatuation? Something connected Zohal to Michael: "Well, teenagers meet, the boy is attractive, and the urge to connect will always be there. "She let her thoughts rest as she mingled with the rest. Maryam had brought special gifts for all. She took Zohal aside, offered her an exquisitely packed box, and said,

"Zohal, baby, open it only when you reach home. I hope you like it. Princesses of our land carried what I am giving you, wherever they travelled."

Zohal was intrigued as to what it would be.

She wanted to see it at once. As she contemplated opening it, her eyes met those of Michael, who was watching her curiosity and gestured to her.

"No, dear."

She was embarrassed.

Michael had chosen the gift, not knowing it would be for the one who would steal his heart. Once home, clutching her precious gift, Zohal ran to her room to unpack it.

"My, it's so beautiful."

It was a hand-held mirror that radiated her beauty in full, like never before. The Aranmula Kannadi, the exquisite mirror made of a secret recipe alloy, that was polished so finely that it reflected the countenance of the beholder, with the inner beauty reflecting alongside. As she read through the description attached to the gift, she realised its uniqueness: it was a craft known only to a few, the recipe handed over generations in the lone family, the official mirror makers, to the royals.

Zohal, the princess, she mused with pride.

Peddling through the streets of Karachi on the bicycle that his brother had gifted him, Michael stopped by the British Library on his customary visit to pick up the latest recommendations to read. He had gotten tired of the Shakespearean-era sagas. As he walked past the reception in search of new launches, he was struck by the sight of the gaiety walk of a girl with her hair dancing in tango with the winter breeze and a clutch of books held tenderly to her bosom.

"Isn't *that Zohal?*"

How could he ever not recognise the girl who stole his heart in an instant?

"Even from the clouds far above, I'll recognise my love, turning into a hawk that could spot a rabbit from miles above".

He lunged towards her, only to be pulled back by the ego of eagerness that would expose his deep desire for her. He did not want to lose her with a bad move.

Michael glanced at what Zohal was reading. It was poetry, and she did have a liking for the Orient. He winced his eyes. It was Tagore, Rabindranath Tagore, the dreamy-eyed poet whose words flowed from the heart, drenched in love with innate humaneness in every couplet.

The Nobel Laureate emanated the calmness that of a yogi. It had the soothing comfort of a mother's embrace or a lover's caress that cascaded through his poetry.

"At the immortal touch of your hands,
My little heart loses its limits in joy and gives birth to an utterance ineffable." - Gitanjali

Zohal had just started with Gitanjali. She was so engrossed in it that she did not notice the presence of Michael, a whiff away from her flowing hair. As she finished the verse and turned, there he was. In a stupor, her eyes dug deep into his.

She was so glad to see him.

As they walked to the cafeteria, she was immersed in the eloquence of Michael, who had completed reading Gitanjali before he turned eighteen. He not only knew the verses but could sing them like a ballad, his recital emanating deep inside with its soul-searching emotion.

She was spellbound.

This time it was Zohal who had the thunderbolt moment; her heart thumping and head spinning, she knew she had met her lover. Looking into her eyes, which were blue with a tinge of green, as on the wings of the peacock dancing in the sun-laced rain that gave it the rare blue-green hue, Michael wanted to immerse himself in her. It was a dizzying moment for both.

They held hands and walked in to wilderness.

Zohal and Mike would meet every week in their cocooned world, sharing their intimate moments.

And then, the tragedy struck. It was so abrupt. The events that unfolded were the worst Michael had feared for his brother.

Paul had a miraculous escape from the crossfire he was caught in. While fighting the Japanese, sixteen members of his team were taken captive and held hostage behind enemy lines. They feared they would be killed the next day as no help was in sight. The night looked never-ending; sleep had taken wings and flown.

Paul's hair turned all grey that night.

That's when it all happened. A counter attack with the Japanese scurrying for cover. All ran out into the crossfire; a shell exploded nearby, piercing Paul's back. He lay in a pool of blood, his eyes blurring. He knew no more.

Thirteen of his team perished.

The soldiers who picked him up from a pool of blood could not believe he was alive. There was a deep and long gash behind his back that extended from his right shoulder to left hip. Paulose had to be airlifted for better care, or he would die.

Michael clutched his brother's hand as he entered the air ambulance, his clutch of pact,

"We *live together, brother."*

To Michael, there was nothing more precious in the world than his brother's life. Semiconscious, Paul returned his brother's call to life clutch with a twitch of his finger. A smile sprouted on his face.

That was the moment the god of death decided to bid farewell.

Michael could not even bid goodbye to Zohal.

Zohal was pregnant.

She knew she would have to raise her love child all by herself.

Will my child ever meet her father?"

"Won't he come searching for his lover, although oblivious of his love child? Or would she travel to his land and be united with him forever."

"But where is his home? Where does his mother live?" She had not asked any of these. In the cocooned world, the cocoon was their universe. The sun rose and set there. The moon was an eternal companion. She consoled herself, saying Mike would come back.

Michael never came back.

Chapter 7
Smile Enigmatic

Those who had seen him and his father together could not have missed the similarity: Mohan's smile was as though it was plucked from his father and stitched onto his lips.

Engaged in an eloquent debate with the young legislators of Kerala in the capital city of Trivandrum,

Mohan argued, "We engineers transform the world. The ideal system of an all-pass-through to final year has changed this year."

"What does it serve?"

"Does it mean that a good portion of the engineers of yesteryears were bad? All we ask is do not replace the good with bad.

Sivadas, the young leader, could not miss the smile, still etched in his memory as an early school student in Malabar. His father was part of the team that was implementing the biggest irrigation project in Malabar. A dam across the river, born in the rain forests of western ghats, one that cascaded the fiery Kakkayam waterfalls nestled in the clouds, that meandered its way to the Arabian Sea.

"The rogue has not lost his fiery speech and the naughty smile".

"What a way to meet the fellow bencher",

But for the smile, Sivadas would have never recognised the jeans-clad hippie.

Sivadas was convinced that Mohan was destined for a path beyond engineering—that of a political activist.

However, knowing that his beliefs were inherited from his father, the only thing he was wary of was whether his foray would catch any moss as it traversed the villainous waters of the politics of the state.

But he wanted him to take the plunge.

"The cesspool needs to be cleaned, and I could be his Kuchela, the classmate of Lord Krishna, if not Chankya, the supreme strategist who launched Emperor Chandragupta."

He mused.

By the beachside at Beatles the Shack, they relived their school life. The album playing *'I wanna hold your hand'* had Mohan take the stage with his McCartney swag.

Soon he had the place swamped with semi-clads swaying to his tune.

Sivadas shed his politician's garb and drank till he dropped. By the time Mohan carried Sivadas piggyback to the nestle, the waves had taken up the song as their own.

Meanwhile, destiny was playing out.

Mohan was a few moons older than his classmates at college, having shed two years while being accepted to Lovedale, the school for the rich, founded by the British more than a century ago.

He had always wondered why the place was named Lovedale.

He recalled the moment they landed at the school as kids. A look at the verdant settings of the school, and a butterfly fluttered in him. For him, it was love at first sight—the love for the verdant settings—that would last a lifetime.

Meanwhile, Salim found the fillies of the mountain school the reason for its name and his instant love for it. The love for the fillies and Lovedale faded into oblivion as he left the school.

It was a rare event of a twins to win the scholarship at the same time for the Eton of Asia. Most in the neighbourhood were in disbelief at the fortunes of Eliza. They wondered why these two were favoured for a life so different from theirs.

Eliza loved listening to these gossips and would taunt a few in favour of what they said, only to secretly vie with her own inner belief that her twins would go places.

On the first day to college, Mohan walked in well-heeled. He had the grandpa umbrella as a constant companion, one that could be construed a style statement or seen as the sword of Ninja, thwarting rain and sun.

Those who saw him were bemused, and he, in turn, could not puzzle out where he had landed and what would follow now.

Mohan read Malayalam poetry but could hardly speak in full earnest in it. He longed for someone who would let him speak in colonial lingo to his heart's content.

Finding it arduous and heart-aching, he decided to ace Malayalam.

"After all, it's my mama tongue," He did it with elan, now equally eloquent in everyday language as well as the foreign lingo.

Soon he discerned that he could recite the deeply anguishing poems of the famous poet Kadamanitta penned in his native tongue with the equal ease as the cooing of love couplets by Pablo Neruda, that touched heart deep.

At the college festival, he sang the Neruda as his own.

"And I love your body of skin, of moss,
of ardent, constant milk.

Ah, the chalices of the breasts!

Ah, the eyes of absence! Ah, the roses of the pubis!

Ah, your voice is slow and sad. Body of my woman, I will persist in your grace.

Even those who did not follow his words were fascinated by the intensity of the recital.

"Was it the angst of a lover abandoned or the cooing of the cuckoo searching for his lover?"

They did not know where he would find it, and even if he did, how would they converse in full earnest? Won't it be a mere attraction of body if his the lovebird could not speak his language like him?

Daisy had just joined.

She had kept aloof as her plan was to get a transfer of studies to the capital city, where her dad stayed.

She had strayed to the festival. Almost bored to the hilt, she had decided to return to her nest of solitude when the Neruda poem floated through the air and caressed her like the morning breeze laced with passion. She had not expected such rendering where she had joined. After all, it was a quaint village from where she had decided to escape, as the place would be drab.

The Neruda poem stirred her.

It awoke her desire and touched her womanhood like no one ever had. Suddenly she craved to know and meet the reciter, the poet, who so eloquently put her feelings into his words.

She slipped into her sleep with those alluring thoughts.

Dy Chief Minister Mathen was the chief guest at the college fest award function. Mohan knew him through his father, who had similar political leanings as his. But he did not want to use his father's connection to meet the de facto kingmaker in the cabinet. Of course, while he knew him, the minister had no means of knowing him.

When the Minister expressed a desire to meet the festival champ, it was a rare honour. Mohan was excited that he would be able to mention his father, and he hoped that the Minister would reciprocate his father's affection for him.

As Mohan walked into the principal's chamber, it was all smiles. The warm embrace of the Minister, Mathen Sir, as he was popularly known, surprised him. The crowd standing in witness to it was in a stupor of the moment.

The icing was when he spoke to all those gathered, holding Mohan close to him.

"Do you know that Michael Sir, Mohan's father, is my alter ego? What a way to meet his son, who's done us all proud by winning the national scholarship."

Mohan felt so humbled.

The stature of his father suddenly loomed over him large. He wanted to run to him and cling to him.

As the minister walked to his cavalcade, he called aside Mohan and spoke with sincere intent.

"Mohan, follow your heart. You have the lineage to make a difference."

Those words coming from the behemoth of Kerala politics were the best gift he had received in a long time—a reminder of what he was capable of and what he may be destined to achieve, provided he seized it.

As he walked the Dy CM to the waiting car, he could not miss the sight of a cheerful girl who walked alongside the minister, a newcomer to the college. Mohan was keen to know who she was.

In the thick of college politics, which was turning turmoil and the din of the university cricket tournament that was on, the search for the girl ceased.

To Daisy, it was love blossoming.

Youngest in the family, a pet of her dad, she hardly had an opportunity to see the world, but through the eyes of her father. She studied at an all-girls school that gave her special privileges, being the chief's daughter.

Everything was so well cared for at home that the rare sleepover at her good friend's place seemed like heaven. It was only at college, staying in the hostel, that she experienced what it was like to be uncaged.

To be a free bird.

Lured by the ballad of Neruda, Daisy was love struck the moment she saw Mohan. For the first time, she felt a flutter in her heart. The butterfly with in took wings in broad daylight to flutter and perch on the lips of Mohan as he stood mesmerising the audience with his recital.

The only time that she had felt romantically inclined was during the rare sleepover with Nadia. Chirping into the night, they would caress and softly kiss to sleep. She found that strange, but nice and soothing at the same time.

But this was love.

And now, knowing that he's dad's good friend's son, there was no way she would let him be someone else's.

"Mohan is mine." Daisy murmured.

※※※

Chapter 8

The Departure

Mohan was distraught when he learned that Daisy had taken a transfer of college and left. It pained him. He felt deceived. "How could she do it without even saying goodbye?" He asked as his thoughts raced. It must have been in the offing for some time, as it cannot be done in a day. It grew on him, whether her feelings were genuine or just a fleeting flirt; for the girl he knew would never do that.

As images of their time together flashed in a replay of the moment, it conflicted with the reality of the instant.

Mohan was accustomed to adoration, but Daisy was a different experience. She had captured his heart in a way that no one else did;—the way she made him feel, be seen, and be understood. He yearned for her laughter; he wanted to be in her arms.

He let his pang linger to know if the feelings were mutual.

Early in to his engineering career, Mohan knew he could never be a rocket scientist. He was an accidental engineer, and his passion lay in management and political science. He had decided to follow one of these after graduation. The following summer, Mohan landed modern history at Jawaharlal Nehru University (JNU).

He loved it.

JNU was a sea of change, from the verdant, quaint village to the bustle of New Delhi.

It brought back memories of his school days where the gifted were respected. The discussions and debates had an intellectual aura that he had missed among the engineering wizards; the bonhomie making up for all that.

He became sanguine at JNU; he was slow to choose friends or have friends choose him. As time passed, Daisy faded from memory, and the pang was reduced to a pinprick that stayed as a reminder of her.

The experience at JNU helped him discover a different facet of himself. The soliloquy excited him more than weekend parties that would see dusk the next day.

JNU had students from all walks of life, and from different countries, many of whom were destined to make significant contributions to their land as political and thought leaders. In the thought-stimulating environs of JNU, they would hone their skills and firm up their beliefs.

Some of these friendships were destined to be part of Mohan's life. One of the closest among them was the bespectacled Abhijit Banerjee, who had a contagious smile and a burning passion for social justice. Coming from a wealthy family in Bengal, Abhijit was deeply committed to improving the lives of the underprivileged.

His discourse, 'Trapped in the vicious cycle of poverty, for life' was a touching essay on the feudal culture that prevailed in most of the north and east of India.

He would argue, *"It's a slave life."*

"One that goes beyond generations. Even the eighteenth-century blacks of America had a route to escape slavery, but in modern India, there was none for these hapless people."

It was a revelation for Mohan that such atrocities still existed in free and modern India, the largest democracy that was awaiting the birth of the twenty-first century.

It was appalling!

He remembered his father's words, a reminder of what independent India had become.

"The viceroy's palace was dirty-big, built to remind the crown that the East India Company sustained her. The lone difference post independence was that colour of the occupant, was different, either brown or black".

"The pomp and regalia had not diminished an iota".

Mohan wanted to know what could be done. He decided to study the transition of bureaucracy from the days of the British as they alone could make a difference.

It was startling to note the decay that had set in bureaucracy. Soon he gathered that but for the islands of excellence of a committed few, the bureaucracy would have imploded into dark abbeys of self-service.

Indian Civil Service ICS had become Indian Administrative Service IAS; post independence, the civil coinage bartered with administrative that did away with the civil servant adage.

It reflected in their thinking and actions glaringly.

"You can only be an administrative master and not an administrative servant, as it's against the basic structure of the English language and its true ethos".

"We will administer like true masters over our servants."

This was now the coveted pledge of service that the civil servants took at the passing-out bash that lasted till all were drunk and knocked out. Many men and women would be in a deep embrace, the power couples of the civil service of the future born then and there.

Mohan had witnessed first hand the power brokering that happened in Delhi. It was the bane that spread its tentacles everywhere. He realised the need for a true transformation and that how activism had the power to drive and make it happen.

As he explored the landscape of the campus that had the budding political leadership of the country his fellow mates, Mohan's own convictions began to take shape. Left-leaning ideology was dominant within the political spectrum. Right-wing thoughts were also gaining ground. He did not align with either. He saw himself as a liberal thinker.

His concept of the role of government as a facilitator and enabler of progress clashed with prevailing regulations and controls that stifled growth. Soon, Mohan became a fresh voice in the sea of political debates, challenging the status quo and advocating meaningful change.

He saw the bloated and decaying civil service as a key factor in the hindrance to progress. They were serving themselves, as per the wish of his political masters than being bound by the oath of service that they took.

Mohan believed that politicians needed to change first, for which principled leaders in the style of Michael had to take centre stage. He was determined that his voice would be heard.

Mohan became aware that life had much more to offer than dwelling on past heartaches. The idealist Michael was being reborn—one who would definitely en-cash the blank cheque to power when the opportunity arrived, unlike his father.

Was destiny playing out?

✳✳✳

Chapter 9

Amsterdam Calling

Far away in her lonely world, Daisy could not help but question her actions.

"Did I hurt him so deeply that we are absolute strangers now? Why have I not had even a reach out from him?"

As the realisation dawned that she was on the verge of losing him, it reverberated back like a hammer boom.

She was grief-stricken.

Daisy never intended to leave Mohan.

She was just unsure about the future of their relationship. In the uncertainty of teenage love, doubts often cloud judgment. With his charm, he could have any girl as his lover.

"Am I good enough?"

The self-doubt was hastened by his sudden departure for the summer project; her fears mounted as he remained unreachable. He had said he would be in the wilderness of the mountains, where he had no means of communication with the outside world.

"But he could sure have kissed a wildflower and sent it with the pigeon."

She had to be sure of his feelings for her.

She rued her impetuousness; the longing just refused to die down.

It was the final semester. Her father had already finalised plans for her. He had set sights on a young IAS officer, Jacob Pothan, who not only showed great promise as an officer but was also from a wealthy and respectable Syrian Christian family.

Her father envisioning a safe and comfortable future for his daughter, where she would marry a man who would ascend to the highest echelons of power in bureaucracy having topped the civil service.

Daisy knew her objections would hold no sway in the matter, as it *was not a my-princess-wish*. Her father's word was the law in the matter.

When her father asked what birthday gift she wanted, she just smiled. He had just delivered a gift that she despised. Her heart yearned for Mohan, her lover.

"Give me Mohan as my birthday gift, papa".

The voice was silent, but she was happy that she spoke her mind. Meanwhile, she couldn't help asking in jest how her new suitor would be. "Would he be a virgin?"

The wedding was pompous. The Prime Minister, too, had sent a special messenger with an invitation for the newlyweds to visit him. After all, Mathen Sir was the kingmaker in the cabinet. He could be useful to Delhi too.

Mohan, too, was there, now a political strategist and thought leader. He had a special gift for Daisy: a white muslin Jamdani sari and a book on the tantric way of life.

"Is he teasing me again or playing a cruel joke".

Either way, she was elated.

As the din of the wedding died down, the newlyweds bid farewell to their guests. It was difficult for both on the first night of a contractual alliance, sans love.

Jacob opened the champagne bottle kept for the occasion, to be popped and drenched in.

He poured the first glass for her and, with a warm hug, led her to the corner foyer that had the Italian sofa facing the thicket of the open garden.

Placing the wine glasses on the ledge, he took her face in his hands. She found the touch warm and comforting. Daisy noticed his look was one of kindness and compassion.

Was there desire too?

"Daisy, *darling.*"

He began,

"I cannot lie to you anymore; I cannot father a child."

That night, Daisy and Mohan made love, like the celestials.

She left for Amsterdam the following day, pricing her pound of flesh for keeping the secret. A seat for Mohan in the ensuing election and a ministerial berth.

Her father was to ensure both.

Daisy was not to return to her land again.

But she knew she would not miss her homeland, which she loved so much, as she was carrying the ethos of her land deep inside.

And a piece of the love of her life with in!

✷✷✷

Chapter 10

The Swearing-in

As he was being sworn into the cabinet headed by 'Leader', the colossus of Kerala politics, he yearned for his dad to be there. It was his dream that he was playing out—the man who could even have been the leader had he agreed to switch sides in the election he fought. Mohan wondered if his father had connived with the gods to transfer his destiny to his son.

Keeping emotions aside and glancing at his supporters that thronged the hall, he repeated the words of the governor in a resolute, never-before-calm tone.

"I, *Mohan Panackal Michael, swear in the name of God."*

The audience stood still in awe at the presence of the young legislator who had trounced the local communist stalwart.

It was justice turning a full circle, he realised.

The hall exploded in applause as he finished. He was mischievously amused that even the Chief Minister, who had led the election from the front, did not get his quantum of applause.

While supporters and family vied to embrace him, he yearned for Daisy. He missed her disrobing smile that made them instantly naked in the midst of crowd merriment. He knew she was the reason he was standing there. After all, how could the supreme head of the party refuse his darling daughter, his princess?

Little did he realise then the impact of 'her pound of flesh pact'.

Mohan had realised the importance of a favourite tag early in life. How much better the other siblings did, it was the eldest who was the father's pet. Mothers, for some strange reason, loved the last one most and may be concerned about what awaits them in a large family.

Knowing her children, Eliza was concerned.

"Will his brothers embrace him or trample him?"

"Well, they were worthy of trampling", she contented.

The years of Malabar life had taught her survival skills. She was no longer the lovelorn naive who craved for Michael, only to be deceived in love.

She chose her lastborn—to be cuddled, protected, and made fit—to fight her brothers in Dharma. 'She would carry him in her womb till her death!'

Passion and desire gave way to love and trust that he got only from one person, his twin brother. He searched for him, well aware that he would not be there, but at this moment he longed for him more than any other soul to be there in witness.

How could we grow so apart?

In their mother's womb, they shared an intimate embrace—an embrace of life and survival. Salim's cross embrace was so warm and most assuring, a perfect union of mind and body that said,

"We will conquer life together."

Unaware to Mohan, Salim and Xariah were watching the spectacle from the corner of the hall.

Amar perched on his father's shoulder, witnessing the birth of a star, the moolam star-born twin of his father. One who would rule as Eliza's trusted astrologer had professed.

✳ ✳ ✳

Chapter 11

My Life, My Love

Xariah left for a winter vacation to be with Zohal-Ama. Salim wondered whether Tamzin was her mother or Zohal.

"Tamzi *is my best friend, and Ama is my soul mate.*" she would say. It made sense; Tamzi too was a teenage mother, which is quite common in Pakistan. Tamzin passed off as her sister most of the time, much to her exasperation. Tamzin loved it and would wear dresses as fashionable as hers to her friends' parties only to tease her. She loved the envious look of her daughter, only to take her in her arms and say,

"I heard that bloke ask, 'How come there is a twenty-year difference between the sisters?'"

Xariah would laugh all the way home.

"Soul and best mate done; I am done, I guess." Salim would ask in fake seriousness. Clinging to him wanting time to stop, she would gleam,

"You are *My Jaan, My Jaanu*;

My Life My Love."

As he dove deep into research, he could not shake off memories of his childhood experiences with his elder brothers. The thrust behind him as they bathed together, the hot bloat demeaning. He wanted to know if those moments of intimacy had a scientific or socio-behavioural answer to them.

It unsettled him.

"I want answers, and who else is better than Xariah?"

She was majoring in psychology, and she could help him understand the madness of this action. In that moment of despair, he yearned for her touch, her voice of reason, and the solace she provided.

When Xariah returned to Boston after the winter break, she dove straight into studies. It was the final term. Salim returned from his week-long research trip three days after Xariah had arrived. He was not aware of her return; the start of post-winter classes was a fortnight away.

He felt lonely and craved,

"Hey, if I wind the clock needle myself, will the days dusk faster and the nights dawn early?"

He wanted her beside him.

Knowing Salim had returned, Xariah decided to shock-surprise him. As she rang the bell, Salim was startled to see her. He had no clue about her early return. In childlike joy, he exclaimed,

"So *my clock trick worked.*"

They kissed passionately, bringing all the missed moments back in a gush of lust and emotions, waking up in each other's arms in a glued embrace the next morning.

Over a cuppa, Xariah listened intently as Salim poured out his thoughts and confusions. Sharing specifics of his research on the phenomenon of attraction, he wanted an answer to his childhood experiences and the questions that plagued him. Xariah listened intently, her gentle demeanour showing understanding and offering comfort.

"Salim, what you experienced with your brother is complex. Intimacy between siblings can be an expression of deep affection."

"For example", she continued,

"Making love is the most intense expression of affection."

Salim nodded, his mind absorbing her words.

"The concepts of moral standards are man-created to suit them, the all-brawn and weak-minded, in tackling their emotions, all in favour of the adult man. Women and children were always at their mercy." she paused,

"I can say with utmost confidence that your brother was subjected to an even deeper experience than what you have experienced, but he in all probability probably enjoyed the act. It would have filled a void for physical intimacy that he yearned for, as a child".

"For him, there is no moral standard to go by."

In an instant, it all started making sense.

"It was only once that I encountered it. Soon after, he came to Malabar to be with the family. Yes, it was the first time I met him at my memorable age".

Left to the care of his grandparents, he never got the love of his mother, which he later confided in Salim.

His heart was lighter now. He could forgive his brother in an instant.

Salim could not stop admiring Xariah's depth of knowledge and knife-sharp analysis of the situation.

"Man, she's gonna go places."

"My lovebird, this thesis is dedicated to you!" He crooned as he held her close to him.

✹✹✹

Chapter 12

Love Child

Salim was racing against time on his dissertation. His guide and mentor, Professor David Heinemann, was upbeat about the project. A doctoral thesis of this magnitude was quite rare, and David decided to spend more time with Salim to hone and fine-tune it for an early completion.

The research was at an advanced stage of testing the hypothesis for its efficacy and validating it through structured observation and trials. This meant Salim spent day and night at the clinic, with an occasional rush home for a shower and some sleep. He had shut himself off from friends and family, turning incognito. But for an occasional call to his mother, he was almost invisible to the rest of his personal world.

Xariah, too, had been through sixteen-hour schedules for weeks now. It drained her and showed on her. She had turned pale, with the irregular eating habits adding to it. Her body started revolting, even rejecting some of the food she used to crave for

"I need some rest and sleep. I need to spend a day on Salim's lap.

Excusing herself from the session, Xariah went home early. Exhausted, she slumped to the bed, sleeping through the day. Rejuvenated, she grabbed her energy drink, Darjeeling tea, specially curated by her grandmother, and walked to the balcony, witnessing the sun turn orange. It reflected off the orange-colored Amphi buses rolling into the water with sway and emerging from it like large turtles ready to give birth.

"How would a baby Amphi turtle look?" she mused.

That's when it dawned on her,

"My, it's been three months now since the last cycle! I have missed it."

She clutched her underbelly in disbelief. Fear gripped her. She had always been careful during the ovulation periods, but how then? The night with Salim, celebrating the return from winter break, was the D-day. Clasping her head in fear and despair, her head spun clueless as to what next. She had to have it confirmed.

Xariah, clad in her casuals, walked to the university clinic, open through the night and day. She knew Ayaan, the young medical intern who had arrived the previous year from Nigeria. True to her name, she was a cynosure to the eye, like a flower bud. She always smiled, and that smile soothed her. Taking her to the corner of the room, Xariah held her hands as if in prayer and said,

Ayaan, I fear I am pregnant.

And I am not even engaged to the guy!

Giving her a reassuring warm hug, Ayaan led her inside the clinic and stood with her all through the procedure. As the lines emerged, Xariah was not sure what they meant. Ayaan looked at it, smiled, and led her to her cabin. Xariah felt relieved; the smile, the most assuring she had seen in the world, meant it was a false alarm. Xariah sank to the clinic chair with a sigh, clutching her face with both hands, letting the mind and body sync in relief.

She went back to her room for some cheese and wine.

The yearning for Salim subdued too.

Ayaan had first met Xariah at the welcome party as an intern. Since then, they have partied a couple of times but never had the opportunity to visit her apartment. She thought,

"I need to visit my friend in her own confines, in the place that would be most comfortable to her. I did not even have time to look into her eyes and see the depth of her feelings."

Xariah was happy when Ayaan came that evening, unannounced. Preferring to sit inside, Ayaan came straight to the point:

"Xariah, you are going to be a mother."

Bolt out of the blue; it took some time for the words to sink in. Her worst fears had come true. She wondered what the comforting smile at the clinic was for, and as she looked up at her, it was still planted there. Holding her face cupped in her palms, Ayaan said,

"Xariah, my friend, isn't this the most beautiful moment in a woman's life—the moment she becomes a part of the universe and eternity by giving birth to a child that's every inch a part of you?"

As she said those words, tears of joy rolled down her cheeks. Xariah could fathom the beauty of the moment only then. She laughed and cried in ecstasy and broke into a tango with her friend, which seemed stellar.

Late after his session with David, Salim was surprised when he saw light in the apartment. And he could not believe his eyes as he saw Xariah in the kitchen. Salim thought

"Xariah had never used the keys to the pad; it's been over six months now that I gave it to her; more to ravish it when I am away."

"What's going on"?

Salim tiptoed to her and held her in a warm embrace from behind. To his surprise, she was not startled but was as in waiting. She turned around and embraced him tightly. Even before he could take her lips, she led him to the sofa in the most lit part of the room.

There was an uncomfortable silence that followed. Salim was worried, as every time Xariah was here, she would fly into his arms, and now it was cold, not even lukewarm.

He looked deep into her eyes, searching for her soul. He could not comprehend the message; it was really deep. As he closed his eyes in thought, he heard a soft voice.

"I am pregnant."

Salim could not decipher what was said. He cupped her cheeks and asked, "What was that?

Tears rolling down her cheeks in a rapid, trembling voice, she said,

"I am going to be a mother, Salim."

As the words settled in, it was as if it was a moment he was waiting for.

"The institution of marriage was a facade for sex; true love comes from a relationship that expects nothing in return but more of love, with the freedom to part when that burning love vanishes". "I want to father my child thus".

Salim carried Xariah to the recliner, kissed her, and crooned to her.

"Darling, our love child."

Salim had had quite a few hedonistic affairs that did not stand the test of time and numerous one-night stands that dissipated into oblivion the next morning.

Finally, the Casanova was tamed.

Xariah travelled through his veins to embrace his heart in love, merging her soul with his. It was the moment of truth for Salim.

Keeping aside all engagements, Salim had Xariah move in with him. He wondered whether his father had the same welling emotion when he was conceived.

Maybe for his eldest. Was he with Eliza at each of her big moments? He wanted to give

Xariah all that she wanted—what his mother may have missed.

Xariah's mind was filled with longing to break the news to Zohal.

"How would she take it?"

Will it be taken as the callousness of a juvenile mind—an unwed mother with a man of another faith who's yet to propose to her? The memories of her grandmother's life bared before her, the trauma, and the upheavals she went through The life of solitude she confined to herself for her child

Will Ama accept me and my child?

Thoughts racing, she decided to call and break the news to Zohal. After all, she was her guardian angel. Facing the orange glow of the setting sun, she called Zohal. Unsure how to start, she closed her eyes, embraced her like only she could, and poured her mind out.

It had no start, no finish; it was a deluge of joy. As she paused, she realised there had been no response from Zohal all along. It surprised her.

"Ama, are you there?"

"Yes, my child."

The voice sounded angelic, comforting her in a way only her Ama could do. She became a butterfly in her cocoon, hibernating like a baby in the womb; her child was cuddled safely inside.

Zohal was not prepared for this.

She was surprised that things went this far. Xariah was no kid, and how could she let this happen—that too in the midst of her defining times? More weird was that she had met Salim only a few months ago. Did she even have time to get to know him well?

It was unsettling.

As she paced for answers, Michael's face loomed large over her. A butterfly fluttered within as the moment of their first gaze came back.

"I guess history is repeating itself."

She philosophised,

"The budding of romance is a wonder that has never been explicitly explained. Why does your heart flutter as you enter your teens? It's so transformative that the boy next door suddenly made you go weak on your knees. It was pure magic, if not the greatest wonder of the world, much taller than all human edifices erected."

She smiled,

"Ahh, Xariah had her thunderbolt moment, just like I had mine decades ago."

Zohal, getting her thoughts together, told herself,

"I have to take Xariah into my hands, and just like I carried her mother in my womb, hold her to my bosom till the safe birth of her child."

"Xariah, sweetheart, Ama needs to be with you at this moment. You will take the next flight out. I am having the tickets sent across."

"Give my regards to Salim."

The line snapped. Xariah was surprised at the suddenness with which the conversation ended. More bizarre was her asking to come immediately.

Still in a stupor over Ama having accepted her, the queer command to visit her while in the midst of the peak semester confounded her, so she walked to the apartment to meet Salim.

It was with difficulty that Salim had convinced David to take a sabbatical to be with Xariah.

And when he heard of the strange demand from Zohal, he was confused and felt cheated.

"It's our child; it's our life. I won't let you go anywhere." were Salim's firm words.

Xariah, looking into his eyes, repeated his words, adding

"My love, I am not going anywhere, but should I not listen to the voice of my angel mother? Just a week, my sweetie pie."

"How long can I live without your cuddles?"

The flight to Karachi was early in the morning. She had packed just a week's essentials. As she waved Salim goodbye, she could see the pain of separation in his eyes. Xariah ran back to be in his hands, kissed him deeply, and took half his angst away for her to keep.

She then did not look back for she knew she would not take the flight home if she did.

✳✳✳

Chapter 13

Birth on Wings

Iqbal, the family driver, was waiting to receive Xariah. As a practice, no one from the family comes to the airport to receive arriving guests. The family preferred to wait at home to welcome their dear ones coming from far away. It was the privilege of Iqbal to do so.

"I was hoping Ama would be here."

She said to Iqbal as he received Xariah and lugged her suitcase into the car. Iqbal looked up, confused, and said,

"You know, princess, I alone come, even when your father comes."

In an instant, she realised she had spoken her yearning out loud.

"Did Iqbal notice?"

He was shockingly confused. It sure showed on his face. Xariah was quiet all the way home. What happened to the chirpy Xariah? Iqbal wondered. Although he wanted to, he did not have the heart to start a conversation to seek answers. He knew something big was occupying her mind.

As Xariah stepped out of the car, her mother enveloped her in an embrace, never wanting to let her go.

"I've missed you, my dearest."

She whispered, her voice choked with emotion.

"We leave for our mountain home early next morning. Ama waits for you there."

The journey to the mountain was filled with anticipation.

"How should I face Ama?"

"What would she say? Why was she so abrupt in ending the call?"

Xariah found it intriguing, especially since it was from her guardian angel. She felt lost. She longed for Salim's presence at that moment.

He would surely have a way to handle her grandmother. He would please her, tease her, and let her take off the burden of facing Ama.

She realised the comfort and reassurance that Salim provided her.

As Xariah alighted at the foothills of Zohal's mountain home, she looked up at the winding pathway that could only be done on foot. She had wondered why it was designed that way. Will she be able to climb it at Ama's age? she wondered. As she walked up, the cool breeze that carried the fragrance of flowers wafted through the air, caressing her hair.

"Now I know why: It's to feel the breeze of ecstasy."

Xariah noticed that Zohal was waiting for her at her favourite spot, the gateway to the mountains. She also noticed the pot of tea and the finest chinaware on the stone table, in accompaniment. It radiated the exquisite smell of tea that could be conjured only by her grandmother.

"Is it not the signature blend?"

The one conjured only for me, the recipe she refused to share with her darling daughter.

Zohal would say to her daughter,

"My child, this is my inheritance that I have decided to pass on to your child, skipping your generation."

Tamzi was jealous of being bypassed.

"I am her daughter, and her care for her grandchild should be second to that for me."

But she cherished the way her mother bonded with Xariah. She faked her protest, only to tickle her mother till she fell to the ground in laughter, with Xariah and Tamzi rolling over her in a laugh riot.

Climbing down the steps to receive Xariah, Zohal held her in a deep embrace, feeling her pulse every inch, searching for answers beneath the surface. She closed her eyes in prayer and kissed her deeply, reaching her great-grandchild deep inside the womb in the warmest of embraces.

"My dearest Xariah, my princess."

Her voice was a mixture of wisdom and love.

"Life has a way of weaving its own tapestry, entwining our hearts in unexpected ways. Your journey, though different from what we envisioned, is so beautiful in its own right."

Embrace this miracle. Let love guide you."

Xariah realised that her journey was not just about becoming a mother; it was about her own discovery, and her child too, in every part of it.

As the weeks passed, Xariah's heart brimmed with joy. She could hear life kicking in; she would know when he slept and when he was most active.

"Like dad, like son, the naughty is most active in the darkness of night."

She said it aloud to the amusement of Zohal.

Zohal thought, *"How was it when I was carrying Tamzi? Was it the same feeling? After all, blood transcends."*

As Xariah prepared to welcome her child, memories of Salim's farewell embrace pained her. It was a bittersweet moment. In her heart, Xariah whispered the words she had held in her heart for Salim at that moment:

"I carry you with me, my love. In every beat of our child's heart, I feel you. You are deep inside me like never before."

The ancestral home nestled in the grandeur of the Himalayas had nature's embrace intertwined with the family's deepest emotions and the fondest of memories. The ancient abode stirred with excitement, its timeworn walls resonating with echoes of the generations past. Xariah bathed in its tranquility. She sauntered through the garden, her fingers tracing the petals of the blooming flowers in resonance with the bud flowering within.

It was now time that Xariah knew the history and heritage of her family. Zohal told her stories of her forefathers, the brave and compassionate women and men who sacrificed a lot for others.

The sun that was consort on each of those walking stories would paint the horizon in vibrant hues for Xariah to see. She would sit at length by the window, cradling her growing belly, feeling the gentle caress of sunlight upon her. The flowers, witnessing, would sway in unison.

"A symphony of love, just like the moment I carried my child inside." Zohal mused.

As the moment arrived, the mountains held their breath in excitement for the moment.

Zohal guided Xariah through her journey of birth. The pain of each contraction reverberated in ecstasy through the valley, to be met with the soothing whispers of the wind that caressed her pain away.

In the tender embrace of the mountain, Xariah gave birth.

Zohal, with tears of joy streaming down her cheeks, cradled him proudly, introducing her great-grandson to the world. Sunlight filtered through the window, casting a soft glow on his face.

"How I wish Michael was with me to see his bloodline."

Zohal missed Michael deeply.

Holding the newborn high above her head, Zohal whispered softly into his ears,

"My little prince, you are named Amar. *Amar, the immortal in love.*"

✳✳✳

Chapter 14

The Thunderbolt

Salim's heart ached with yearning to hold Xariah in his arms and to share those precious intimate moments stolen from them. Days turned into weeks and his longing grew deeper, hoping for her return. And then, a few days after their arrival at the tranquil mountain home, Zohal called him. "Son, listen to my words with utmost attention. I understand the ache in your heart and the longing to be with your beloved. But for the sake of Xariah and for the well-being of the seed that grows within her, I must keep her cocooned in the safety of our ancestral abode. It is a tradition, and it is in her best interest."

Salim's frustration began to dissipate as Zohal shared her own journey as a teenage mother raising her child all by herself. Her words painted a picture of resilience, and he understood the need for Xariah to be with Zohal. Traditions had to have the birth at the mountain home.

"I will bring your baby and your beloved to you very soon thereon."

The ache of separation remained, but Salim felt reassured. "Meantime, you get your research completed as a gift to your child." Zohal concluded.

And the day arrived.

Zohal, holding Xariah close to her, handed Amar to the waiting arms of his father. He was fast asleep. *Once in Salim's hands, he stirred awake, his eyes fluttering open to meet his father's gaze.*

Salim leaned forward to kiss his gleeful son on the lips, and their souls merged. As Amar smiled, Salim noticed that his father's smile was for sure inherited by him.

Xariah found everything in the apartment the way she had left it. The only addition was a simple and elegant crib that swung, as though it had welled in the mountain breeze, for Amar to feel at home. It was Zohal's first visit to Salim's apartment. Dressed in a gold-laced suit and sporting dark shades, she looked elegant and radiant.

Salim showed Zohal to her room.

"Ama-Zohal, this room is yours for keeps. Freshen up; I'll get you a hot cup of coffee." She liked the change from the usual tea. Zohal rested her handbag on the table and let her eyes wander the room. The wooden-framed photograph was vintage, and she admired it. Then she froze in the moment. The face she had been searching for all these years.

There he was, wearing the jacket she had gifted him.

It hit her like a thunderbolt. The whelmed emotions of decades came gushing in a deluge. Her head spun. She clutched the frame not to fall.

Zohal looked up into the sky in disbelief.

Her eyes welled in ecstasy.

"Salim's father is my lover?"

The laughter, the tenderness, and the dreams they had woven in each other's arms were all happening once again, all over. Tears rolled down as she traced the contours of her lover's face in the photograph, feeling the weight of their unfinished story filling her heart. It was a secret she had guarded fiercely, a love that had remained hidden in her depths. It was a rendezvous with a portrait that held a thousand unspoken words.

As overwhelming as the revelation was, Zohal knew she had to guard it even more intently now. Michael had moved on with his life, and she could never be the reason for a tremor there. It was the sacrifice she had promised herself she would make in such an eventuality, burying her own burning desires.

Zohal placed the photograph back in a silent farewell to the past.

Salim, you are my unborn son.

She hid her emotions behind her shades as Salim came with the specially brewed coffee.

She placed it on the foyer desk and touched his cheeks in motherly love.

"Thank you, my son."

Oblivious to the depth of it all, Salim embraced Zohal the way he embraced his mother.

✳ ✳ ✳

Chapter 15
Mystical Malabar

As the car took the turn from the main crossroad that took them to Salim's Malabar home, the view was green and the road was newly asphalted. It took a few minutes more to reach the private road up home. Memories that welled had the country road snaking down the hillocks as it travelled home Cutting the mounds to their death, it was a road that had no ups or downs.

The travel was smooth, but Salim was sad.

"What have they done?" He rued. His anger was discernible. "Will you cut the nose or breasts for an easy caress? Weren't those curves a symbol of your beauty and an expression of who you are?"

He felt slaughtered.

Mohan and Salim had joined St. Anthony's primary school at the village square at the age of six, which in those days was deemed the best time for a child to go to a structured regime. Till then, it was life devil and sleep rare for Salim and the obedient and sleep tight for Mohan, being the darling of the family.

In fact, he hardly slept, preferring to have his mother breastfeed him. And the ritual continued till he was an overgrown exploiter, four and a half years old. Had Ayesha not been born that year, in all honesty, he would have had it lifelong.

The spoiled brat

The school had classes till the fourth. Being the twins of Michael, the Headmaster of the apex institution, they did enjoy a special status. The free lunch of upma, a grain concoction made from the American free grain programme, was not one of them, but Salim would do anything for it.

It was yummy.

Mohan preferred lunch at home, and Salim had his own doubts whether that was more to steal Ayesha's milk than the food itself. When she cried, he was gracious enough to let her feed from the other side. No wonder Mohan and Ayesha grew the fondest.

It was only when his father told him that the free upma was for those who could not afford food from home that he knew its purpose. But it was too good to let go; he wanted it and would have it.

Salim asked his mother, "Mama, can I trade it with Pavi four times a week?" Noting the quaint smile as a no, he asked, "Three times a week?"

The smile remained. Mother and son had decided on one day a week and that his father would be kept in the dark for life. Salim never broke that promise, but his class teacher did, and it ended the sweetest savoury the following week. Salim has not forgiven her till now.

The childhood memories whiffing in, Salim did not notice that he had arrived at the foothills of the mound home. On the left, Mummy-Well, named after Eliza, survived the road expansion, offering the sweetest water to all in need, especially the pedestrians who quenched their thirst on the long walk back home.

Lolita was as old as his sister, Ayesha. She had arrived from Michael's village, Methala, along with her mother Paaru, to help Eliza at home. Paaru had a smile sprout right from the moment she woke up and started her chores, which lasted till she slept. Lolita would follow her mother like a duckling behind the mother duck.

She chanced to see how Devon treated Eliza during his most disturbing times, and she was terrified. "If our protector has no solace, what will come to us, Amma?" She would cry, clutching Paaru in fear.

Seeing Devon, she would run behind the kitchen, plucking weeds with her tiny fingers, to escape the wrath of Devon. Reminiscing about the moment, Salim could not control his tears, seeing the shivering little girl's countenance still etched deep in his memory. Salim had to wash away the trauma and pain as a penance for the family.

It was Eliza who took her under her wing to educate her as her own. She was a teacher now, and Salim was carrying a special gift for her.

There were others too in the memorable growing-up period: Govindan the boy, who would spin yarns of his youthful adventures tinged with mischief with older girls. Salim remembered that these tales awakened a curiosity that he couldn't fully comprehend. He found his touch during those stories to be a gentle grace that aroused a peculiar desire for more of his stories. Just as he sprouted, Govindan vanished one day. Salim missed his commedia.

Michael had moved to Malabar soon after the election. Eliza's twins were sons of Malabar by their birthright, conceived there and delivered in Travancore.

Mohan held the nostalgia for Malabar, and he would say, "Salim, you are truly a Travancore soul, with your scheming ways. I am the true son of Malabar."

Salim couldn't agree more. His twin was the gentleman of the two.

A rising political star too.

✻ ✻ ✻

Chapter 16

Forgotten Lives

Michael's move to Malabar coincided with the social churn that welcomed the new state.

The surge to fight the exploitation still faced by the Dalits was evolving. Kerala had a history of long ingrained caste system. Manusmriti, the societal code of conduct among Hindus that favoured the Brahmin, was in practice in Kerala at its height of exploitation.

The Namboothiri were erudite and wealthy. They held sway over society and had the sole right to be priests in temples. Most of the land was theirs, leased for tilling to the lower castes, the Nair and Ezhava. The royals too had a special place for them, paying obeisance to them more out of fear of their wrath than love for them.

Antharjanams, the women of the clan, were perpetually confined to the Mana, the mini castle they lived in. Mana was exquisitely designed with labyrinthine stairways and footpaths leading to the private bathing ghat. The day would begin at the bathing ghat, with maids in attendance massaging them head to toe with scented coconut oil infused with herbs. A sadya, the traditional feast followed by a siesta and songs, completed the routine. Their lives looked blessed, but their faces showed the ignominy.

Namboodiri held significant sway over the lower castes, much like their ownership of land. In the pecking order, Nair occupied the position just below them, thereby enjoying significant patronage. They were the foot soldiers in the king's army. The Namboodiri-Nair association had its own complexities. The matriarchal system, or Marumakkathayam', that had women inherit all the wealth was in vogue in Nair families. The man moved into his wife's house, over which he had no right of possession, after the wedlock.

Women controlled family matters with a vice-like grip that had the husbands receiving what the lady wished to share with them. The lady of the house was a cynosure, with the keys to the locker dangling from her navel. And her voluptuousness held a rare allure for the godly class, Namboothiri.

The sandals at the entrance to the abode foretold that the lady of the house was in rendezvous with her paramour. It was a signal to the husband, who was returning home, to return the next day, and if the sandals were still there, to return again. In those intimate moments, she would sing him songs brimming with passion and feed him a half-chewed beetle leaf concoction laced in tobacco.

Their bodies would then merge.

Each visit made the family richer. The Nair clan was ever grateful to their ladies and the system of matriarchy for their evolution as the new privileged class, even surpassing their own masters.

The lowest caste of Dalits, comprising pulaya, paraya, and similar, were trapped in a situation of extreme exploitation with no escape from it, unlike the rest. Confined to the fields and kitchens as menials, they were denied even basic rights. It was a society in which the Dalits existed only in the shadows, as did the cows and goats back home. Women of their clan were barred from covering their breasts.

Stripped of any dignity, the males bore the shame silently, hapless like the dead. They were untouchables, the impure to be kept at bay. Their touch would make it *ashudh*, or impure, and the sight a curse, forcing them to hide behind the bush or lie face down on the ground to escape being seen as the Namboodiri crossed their path. It was hell on earth for them.

But lust had no such rules.

In the darkness of night, he would search out her hut to feed on her. The fable of Cherumi had Aphan in extreme thirst in the middle of his escapade. Offering him water in a fresh tumbler, he pulled her to him and touted, "Ashudham, your touch has made it impure."

Undeterred by his disdain, she offered again, "Thampurane, my Lord, how else will I quench your thirst, unless, of course, you decide to slurp my body for water till it fills you?" She said, vengeance laced with twinkles in her eyes.

In agreement, Aphan whispered, *"I will drink it from your innermost: your Yoni. Pour it there."*

Spreading her legs wide, she clutched Aphan's head in a wild embrace and thrust it against her pubis. Aphan slurped. His heart pounded in erotic ecstasy, getting deeper and deeper into her. His eyes closed, and as he gasped for air scented with her nectar, he could feel the grip tightening with Cherumi's leg sleuthing like the python around his back.

A grip from which he could not escape and did not want to.

As his nostrils filled, Aphan's heart stopped to remain eternal in her.

Kali-Cherumi lay back, Aphan's head listless, still between her thighs. In the darkness of the night, Karumba, her black cat, and her sole companion cuddled up in witness.

As Aphan was confined to flames, the tale of Kali-Cherumi, the enchantress, drew more to her, like the firefly to the fire.

Each night, she enslaved young Thampuranes of the land, begging to be consumed by her.

It was her sweet revenge.

Revenge for the generations of oppression she and her likes bore.

Chapter 17

Prodigal Son

Eliza's firstborn, Devon, was more handsome than her husband. His smile was genuine, and his dove-tailed eyes radiated compassion.

She was proud that it was her body and soul that gave him that radiance. Her greatest grief was that she was pregnant again and could not give all she wanted to her boy. Soon she had to leave him in the comforts of her parents as she was towed away by Michael to Malabar. Her heart yearned for her boy; the boy missed her more.

The mother, in whose womb he wanted to live his life, left him and went. The next time she came, Eliza was pregnant with her third child. To Devon, she had become distant; his heart could see his mother walk to the horizon without even looking back.

His first poem was laced with pangs and a desire for his mother's embrace. His songs and plays spiced the summer holidays with cousins as actors and the harvested rice field as stage. They were good, really good. He longed for his mother to be there to see it, to embrace him in joy as others cheered. His longing grew old; now he was too big to be held in an embrace by his mother.

He moved to Malabar when he turned sixteen. The tranquility of Malabar was discomforting to him from the luxury of his town life, but he became acquainted with it soon. He was suddenly in a world where all village knew him and he none; for being the Headmaster's eldest son, he was the legend of the land even before his arrival. They had imagined he would be handsome like Michael, but his drooling eyes were a few notches above what his father brought forth.

They just lapped him up.

With time, Devon relished his new-found identity; it helped him overcome the neglect from his mother. As adulation towards him grew, he resented his mother more and more for abandoning him. The newfound power made Devon want to inflict the same pain on his mother.

"It *cannot be just the emotional trauma that I experienced*. She has borne so many after me. If she has to feel it, it has to be a physical expression of the same. A hundred lashes? but where do I get the whip?"

At the height of longing—loneliness—he would drag his mother by the hair on the ground. He would stand there with his leg raised, waiting for her to plead for mercy.

"Forgive your mother, son." Eliza would say within.

"I realise that I failed you. But do you know that my heart still aches every moment, thinking of it?"

Devon would look away and leave silently, as if in full recognition of what she said silently.

In the middle of the night, as the world slept, Devon would slip into his mother's room, clutch her feet in love, and sob, tears washing her feet in repentance. Eliza would lie still, forgiving her son for all he did; in quiet, she would say,

"Maybe I deserved it for walking away from my child when he most needed me. Lord, forgive him for what he does, for he knows not what he does. Forgive me, Lord, for abandoning my child."

Devon wanted to be an actor.

The watershed moment in his life was when his father cold-shouldered his dream of being an actor, taking him to the theatre. He had hoped that his father would embrace his wish for an attempt at admission to the prestigious film institute. But none came.

"Well, if that's his decision, so be it."

He did not even ask his father what his decision was or what he should do from then on.

Michael had become more of a father-in absence, with social and political commitments taking up most of his time. That's when Devon grew close to Eliza. The mother's love, which he so much yearned for but was denied, came back to him in a torrent. He basked in it and whispered, "Mama, I will protect you and Ayesha, my little bird, with all my might."

Michael had his own ill-wishers in the land, where most loved him and a few jealous of him. Chacko was one of them. He lived right opposite their home, with the stream and the paddy fields separating them. A huge rock mound, or 'ppara' in native tongue, stood majestically in between, the stream encircling it while winding down. The giggling waters could be waded to Chacko's house.

Chacko was the first of four siblings. His parents had migrated from Travancore to Malabar in search of better avenues for their family, and they did build a fortune. The house in which Chacko lived was his father's gift; he was a very affable man, very different from his son.

Lanky, rustic, and handsome,

Chacko managed his "arrack" country liquor shop at the village square. Clad in a pressed dhoti and shirt, he would come home every afternoon for lunch, take a brief siesta, and go back to his shop to shut shop and return late in the night. He would be fully drunk each evening. Every night, he would stop in front of Eliza's house and profusely abuse Michael and his family. The blabbering would be indecipherable on most occasions. But it was loud and vitriolic.

Devon wondered, Why this hatred?"

He could get no answer. "Ah, interestingly, it happens only while dad is away." With Michael away for days at a stretch, Eliza got wary of this routine; her daughter Ayesha was old enough to feel the fear. She feared Chacko would harm her mother and might even take her away. She would hug Eliza tightly the whole night, never letting her go.

Devon saw the fear in his kid sister's eyes and the helplessness in his mother.

He decided, "Enough is enough."

That evening, at dusk, Devon walked into the arrack shop with his friend Anthony in tow. Anthony was senior to him and had dropped out after eighth. He now ran errands for his father, who owned a grocery shop. It was empty most of the time. Sitting at a vantage position from where he would be visible to all, Devon ordered a bottle of liquor. The whole village square stood still, in shock.

The Headmaster's son, still in his teens, had become a prodigal, a tippler. The tipplers at the shop suddenly turned silent; they had never witnessed anything like this. It was known that boys of big homes occasionally had it pilfered from partying elders and consumed it in the thickets. That, too, was rare. Here is the handsome young man, son of the headmaster!

The tipplers felt a sense of pride. Here was one who would give them a sense of dignity.

"We are not drunkards any more. We are tipplers who enjoy the fine craft, laugh, dance, and speak aloud. After all, how silent and boring would the world be without us?"

Devon was taken aback by the sudden silence. He was perplexed by the attention and adulation he received. He smiled at all as Anthony opened the bottle and poured his glass, handing it over to him for his first sip.

It was rabid and strong. Devon knew that if he took it, he would collapse to the floor like the dead. He wet his lips with it. He filled his palm pool with the arrack and caressed it over his flowing hair all the way to his shoulder. It was a ritual he had hearted that he would do, one that resonated with the Rishi's accepting the divine offering of gods after penance, eyes in arrogance as if it were their birthright.

"Even *the creator of the universe, 'Brahma', would be wary of inviting the wrath of the Rishis.*"

Rishi-Devon asked the glasses of his admiring tipplers to be filled from his bottle. Walking to Chacko in his seat, he said, "Feed them to their heart's content. They are my followers, and today they need to celebrate."

Throwing the bank notes on the table, Devon grabbed a bottle, took Anthony by his shoulder, and swaggered to the village square and to the cosy comforts of Anthony's foyer.

Chacko never again stopped at Eliza's house on the way back in the night.

Chapter 18

The Lass

Devon despised Thiruthi, the second wife of Cheman, the blacksmith. She was almost his age, maybe a couple of moons more, and was voluptuous. She liked to show it.

Rumours abound that she poisoned her first suitor to be with Cheman, the 'rich' blacksmith of the land who could afford to feed her milk and meat and save her from working all day to earn a living. Anthony would say, "They never married. She's a schemer, Devon."

The story went like this:

In the darkness of the night, Thiruthi sleuthed into Cheman's hut, tore away her clothes, and lay still beside him till dawn. Saroja, Cheman's daughter, would be the first to rise and wake her father up, and there she was, naked, sleeping beside him. Shocked, her cries froze in her throat. Saroja placed the concoction beside him and walked down to the stream through the morning drizzle.

She despised Thiruthi.

Thiruthi did not reciprocate the same feeling. After all, she was her mother now, though only three years older than her.

She would say,

"I have usurped the love of a father for her daughter; I have taken her mother's place too in her father's heart. I need to be kind to her."

Never did Thiruthi confront Saroja, whatever the provocation. She had better things to do.

Devon exploded with rage as she saw Thiruthi walking into his estate to cut fodder grass. He had warned all that it was needed for the cattle at home. He would voluntarily give away anything that could be spared.

"These rules do not apply to me."

Thiruthi would declare to her friends with a sinister smile, chuckling along at the same rhythm as her swaying bosom.

Rushing down the slope, Devon caught Thiruthi with her hair, swung her around, and slapped her to the ground. Writhing in pain, she looked up in bewilderment, then locked her eyes with Devon as an invitation to take her into his arms. As Devon closed his eyes, the sight in the darkness of midnight came haunting. The sight of the black lass tearing into his father on the crevice of the behemoth rock was as if the crevice was born out of the thrust of the lass.

There she lay, wreathing, still inviting. Devon clutched her hair and pushed her to the road, with people watching. "Never again will you set foot on my land, you wretch."

That pained Thiruthi. She felt disgraced.

"He could have beaten me to a pulp; I would have taken each strike as a caress, but this was an insult. Devon Chetta, you have laid your hands on me; you have insulted me as I am a low caste. I'll make you pay for it."

What hurt Thiruthi most was that *Devon was the Adonis of her dreams.*

Chapter 19

Arrest Without Warrant

Sebastian had taken charge that day as the sub-inspector of police at Kayanna police station when Thiruthi came to register her complaint along with the local politician.

Thiruthi wanted to salvage her pride.

As she stated the incident, she grew uneasy. The politician by her side was edging her to press for molestation, adding his own version to the incident. The atmosphere there was unnerving to Thiruthi. There was no lady constable in the vicinity. It looked like a fortified dungeon to her, from which she could never escape.

Sebastian edged on.

It was his first day and the first case. What better way to stamp his mark? It was the most infamous station.

Rightly put the most famous in the state of Kerala. One that changed the course of the politics of the land.

The Naxalite, alias Maoist, movement had found its ethos among the young and educated youths of Malabar. Many were from wealthy families who despised the exploitation and oppression of the Dalits that still prevailed. REC, the engineering college, where the brightest students had a cell that organised resistance, professed the need for oppression to end, and a few were even willing to take up arms.

"After all, it's for the noblest cause. We need no more aphan-namboothiri-likes." They declared.

Mahesh's father was a college professor; Methyl Narayanan had the pedigree of a civil service father. The common ground for both was the despicable exploitation that still existed in Malabar.

The Kayanna police station attack and its aftermath shook the land. The state that had elected the first communist government through the ballot, in the annals of world history, had a communist Chief Minister then, who turned predator to those who held the core of its value to their hearts: proletarian emancipation. It led to the crushing annihilation of the Naxalite movement with extrajudicial execution.

An innocent prey was Mahesh, the bespeckled, soft-spoken brilliant engineering final semester boy who could explain the principles of rockets with the same ease as the rights of people and the need for the outcasts to regain those rights on their own terms.

"It's not a favour we ask for; it's our birthright," he would say.

Those words made a thousand flowers bloom. Not once did Mahesh touch an arm in his life. His most potent arms were his words and his writings. The police snuffed it out in a moment, crushing his limbs under iron rods and throwing the carcass into the Kakkayam waterfalls in the rain forests of Malabar.

The following night, the sky opened up in grief and revenge, flooding the town, holding all guilty of not protecting a brave son.

It took a week for the water to recede.

It's said that even the most genial people turn into a devil as they step into the Kayanna police station in Khaki. Sebastian was not genial, and he turned into a scheming devil with his eye on the Station House Officer (SHO) seat.

"Thiruthi, this is a matter of grave concern, not only for you but for all the well-meaning women of our land. We should and will fix this." He asked his writer to take the complaint in writing and prepare the First Information Report (FIR). The SHO was away.

"Should I wait for his return or go right away and pick up the 'bastard'?" His fist pounded.

As he walked back to the writer's room, he shouted, "Police Constable PC, get the jeep ready, take the handcuffs, double the number of policemen", He felt elated at the possibility of the occasion.

Thiruthi refused to give a statement as asked for. It was clear what had happened. There was no molestation. It was a true expression of his anger.

"I am also at fault that way." She told the writer.

"I trespassed against repeated warnings. I only want him to be spoken to and, if possible, to receive an apology from him. That's all I want."

Sebastian was furious. He dictated the complaint as well as the FIR. Thrusting Thiruthi by the neck, he thumbed her signature and signed the FIR himself. Twitching his moustache, he walked to his vehicle, beckoning others. Thiruthi cried aloud in disbelief. The sane ones around could not fathom what was going on.

"Is the notoriety of Kayanna never going to end? Won't the ghost of Mahesh ever forgive us?" They rued.

By the time Michael got wind of what was happening, the police team had left for his house. It was turning dusk, and he knew where Devon would be: at the local talkies, at the village movie theatre that had the opening of a new movie the same day. His son would never miss a new screening, the first day of the first show, and that too, with his fans in tow. Michael was there before the police arrived.

He waited for the events to unfold.

Screeching his vehicle to a halt with dust on the unpaved floor flying up, masking the sight, Sebastian barged into the cinema hall, shouting for the show to be stopped.

The lights came on. The viewers were shocked to see a platoon of policemen led by a rabbling sub-inspector of police. As he shouted, Evideda: Where the fuck is Devon?

Devon stood up, his friends forming a cordon around him. This infuriated Sebastian even more, as he saw it as defiance, a challenge to his authority. He knew he had to nip it in the bud for his own survival.

He lunged towards the cordon, kicking aside Anthony, who stood in front like a wall. As he raised his hand to lift Devon by the collar, his hands trembled under the aura of the man who rose in front of Devon.

His father Michael.

"You *will not touch my son!*"

The land had never seen this face of him. His eyes pierced, his voice stung; he grew in size to the disbelief of people.

"Inspector," Michael said, calming his voice. "I do not know what you seek my son for. I am not even asking. He will be there at your police station sharp 10.30 tomorrow morning."

Even before Sebastian could gather what was happening, Michael gestured for the rest of the police to leave and asked the operator to restart the movie.

For the first time in their lives, father and son watched a movie together.

※※※

Chapter 20

The Suicide Pact

The duel suicide shook the world. Devon was at his ancestral home when the news was delivered to him by a special messenger.

Listening to it calmly, giving no expression of its severity, Devon walked the messenger to the gate and returned to shut himself in his room. His grandfather knew something was amiss; he waited for his grandson to compose and seek his solace, whatever it was and whenever it would occur.

Biting his palm till it bled, Devon cried silently. Packing his bag, he came out of the room into the waiting arms of his grandfather. He hugged him and said,

"Grandpa, I need to go; I don't know when I'll be back." Avira spoke no words.

He accompanied him to the bus stand, and as the bus moved, he handed him a small packet of money. He knew that his grandson would need it. Devon did not even wave back at his grandfather's goodbye. His eyes were transfixed as if he could see it all happening in front of him. He lost himself in thought at his last rendezvous with Anthony.

Devon had decided to meet Thiruthi once he was told what transpired at the police station. It was not the Thiruthi he had known; better put, he thought he knew. Whatever the provocation, he had harmed her. He had made dust off her soul. He wanted to meet her and say sorry.

Cheman was at his bellow as Devon walked in. Thiruthi was pounding at the hot iron as if in repentance of her action. She stopped and stood up upon seeing Devon, her eyes pinned to the ground. It pained him; the lady who held her head high and gazed into the eyes of anyone she met was a shadow of her past.

Cheman knew this was the moment his wife was waiting for—to bury her grief and have full repentance. Getting up from the bellow, he smiled at Devon, patted him, and walked down to the stream. "They need their time now."

Devon held Thiruthi by the shoulder and made her sit on the bench beside him. He raised her face; it was expressionless, he noticed. He could sense a cloud welling in her, ready to burst.

"Thiruthi, I am sorry, he said. Please forgive me."

Her welled emotions burst. She clutched his feet, pleading for forgiveness. Devon let her cry it out. Once she was composed, he looked into her eyes and said,

"This should be the last time you lower your head and cast your eyes down. Your boldness should inspire your people to live their minds." She nodded, her smile showing the little dimple on one side. Sipping tea that Thiruthi had freshly brewed,

Devon continued, "Thiruthi, I have one more matter to discuss with you, something extremely important. You know the growing affection between Saroja and Anthony. It frightens me."

Thiruthi had sensed it but felt helpless.

"The low-caste girl, courting the son of a Syrian Catholic, the descendant of a respected family of Travancore, if not pure madness, what would you call it?" She had asked herself.

Thiruthi had tried to reason with Saroja, but it was all in vain. As if vengeance were owed to her, their bond only grew stronger. The only thing Thiruthi could do was keep her pet dog in complete silence as Saroja received her lover in the darkness of the night. Thiruthi did not want Devon to feel the helplessness and the truth of the situation. He would be distraught, as she knew how much he loved his friend Anthony. Thiruthi promised to speak to Saroja, fully knowing she would not even give her an ear.

The news of a girl's body floating at the neck of the stream and the body of Anthony hanging from the tallest tree on the hillock behind came at the same time.

It was not two, but three lives that were consumed. Saroja was pregnant sixteen weeks with Anthony's child.

The funeral was over by the time Devon arrived.

Anthony's mother was inconsolable. She clung to Devon in her last hope, pleading,

"Son, ask him to come back. He will listen to you. He did everything you asked him to do. Ask him to come back. I want my son back, Devon."

Devon held her close in a tight embrace until she collapsed in his arms.

Saroja's ashes were kept in an earthen pot bound in red at the entrance to their hut, placed in reverence on the bench. Devon noticed it was the one he had sat in on his last visit. Cheman was at the bellow, air blowing red hot in fury, ready to consume the whole world—the only salvation he saw for his daughter. He did not even notice the presence of Devon as he entered and stood beside him.

Thiruthi had just finished pouring oil into the lamp kept at the head of the urn to have the flickering flame burn brightly. As he closed his eyes in prayer for her, he noticed that there was no one else in the house.

"Has the whole world abandoned them?" Tears rolled down his cheeks.

He cried for the first time since he left his grandfather's home. The angst of neglect was far bigger than the loss of their child.

Seven days later, Saroja's ashes were immersed in the same spot where she was found floating, her last resting home among the midget fish that she used to net, only to be released back, having bonded their friendship. Besides Cheman, Thiruthi Devon was the lone person present.

He floated a bunch of freshly plucked lotus, 'Aaambal, from his garden, bidding her goodbye.

Devon had collected a small portion of her ashes in a gold-laced box that Anthony had kept to buy her sindhur to lace her forehead in crimson, proclaiming their wedlock to the world.

Standing at Anthony's grave in the sheathing rain, he buried Saroja's ashes deep in it, piercing the cask joining them.

In a wedlock of eternal union.

Chapter 21
Zohal & Eliza

To Salim, his mother, Eliza, was his greatest strength and his biggest weakness.

But for her, the twins would have been buried as premature births. She tended them with her soul. Combined with a firm belief in the power of Avira's god, they survived. Deep inside, he knew it was a mother's resolve that got them through.

Eliza knew Salim was coming with his girlfriend. She was happy Salim had found someone who would keep him to herself. The genes having flowed from her husband, she was wary that, outside wedlock, he would father a dozen. Ayesha, his sister, and Eliza were home;

since no intimation of his arrival was given, Eliza was at the farm on the hillock.

For Xariah and Zohal, it was a new experience—a visit to the wilderness of Malabar. The stretch home was a dirt track, which Eliza maintained as a reminder to future generations so that they did not lose sight of the arduous journey that she and her husband took.

It added to the mystique.

The suave Salim, who charmed the scholars of Boston, had his roots here. Both exclaimed.

"That's what makes him stand out," Xariah reminisced. "How little I knew of his roots and the past."

As they walked up the snaking walkway, Ariyan, the caretaker, came running down to hold Salim's hands in visible excitement. Salim took Ariyan in a warm embrace to the confusion of Zohal and Xariah. Their bond dates back to when Salim was seven years old.

"Ariyan must have completed twenty-five years with the household",

He reminisced. Ariyan had an oversee of kids, keeping them safe. His knowledge was far above that of others. Having studied up to eighth grade, he could read and write English. The sudden death of his father forced him to seek a job to tend to the family in his father's absence. He discontinued his studies, but he took a wow that no one else in his family would drop out. He went on to support his brother and sister in their studies and gain jobs in government. They progressed in life, scaling the comforts of it. Ariyan still walked to work four miles a day. He never sought financial support from anyone, including from his brother.

Salim inquired where Mama was. "You know Salim, Balan, and his wife would swallow half of today's pluck unless Mummy kept watch. She's at the farm."

Refraining from calling his mother, Salim decided to go. "You take good care of my guests."

That was when he noticed Xariah and Zohal. In the bewilderment of seeing two fashionable ladies, one clad in loose linen and the other in her comfortable denim, both spotting dark shades, he refused to see the baby.

"So far, so good," Salim thought. "One question less."

Salim walked up the hillock from where the twins used to hurtle down at breakneck speed. The aracanut trees had grown taller. Some leaned in, looking their age.

Eliza was facing away from Salim as he reached the mound. He tread cautiously so as not to have the crackling of twigs deceive his arrival.

Let me surprise her with a deep embrace.

The lack of surprise as he embraced her from behind surprised him. Eliza caressed his cheeks and asked, "Is Xariah tired? Did you have a safe and comfortable trip?

He had planned to startle his mother with his embrace, having advanced the trip by a fortnight and keeping her in the dark. The lack of surprise meant that she knew he was there. "But how? I had tiptoed up the mound, Mama."

"I can sense your body fragrance from a mile away, my son."

Sensing his bewilderment, Eliza said. He kissed her, realising how his life was so intertwined with his mother's. He could feel the umbilical cord rebirth and connect them once again.

One could walk straight onto the terrace from the hillock. Having put Amar to sleep, Zohal and Xariah were being shown the view down the road that ran parallel to the gleaming stream. So engrossed were they in the conversation that they failed to notice Eliza's arrival. Perched above the terrace, he could see a twinkle in his mother's eyes when she whispered to him, "It's *a boy, right?*"

Salim did not know what to say. How on earth would she know Xariah had a baby with him? How could she read that she was a mother? Xariah still looked just out of her teens.

"Son, a mother can read the mind, a lady can fathom another, the subtle differences in contours they draw. I read your mind and saw the hue on, Xariah."

As mother and son walked closer to them, it was Xariah who turned first, looking straight at Eliza, a little startled at her appearance. Eliza, donning a printed cotton sari, held Xariah's face in the softest of fondles. Looking deep into her eyes, fathoming the love she had for her son, Eliza kissed her cheeks.

"Welcome my child, Xariah. Salim has chosen well. You are the pearl we were waiting for."

Xariah's green eyes gleamed in the rays that impaled the cloudy sky. Zohal was in deep anticipation of this moment: *How would Eliza look? Will I match her in looks? Has Michael fallen for the colleen more charming than her, the irresistible one?*

Zohal was observing the meeting of his granddaughter with Salim's mother. Eliza had the aura of a mother, not only to her children but to the whole precinct. Her eyes were kind but had melancholy in them. She was brown with a rounded face, and her body had worn beyond the age on her face. She dressed simple, and it was a surprise to her, knowing the rich taste that

Michael had for clothes. She still cherished the black and gold gown that he had presented to her.

"Those were the days when we preserved the best for each other." Zohal felt disappointed with Michael.

"This is no way to attire your love. Maybe he did not love her deeply enough like he loved me. Or did he, and if so, why did he not come searching? He could have easily found me." Zohal's heart raced.

As Eliza's eyes met those of Zohal, she was still holding Xariah in a warm hug. Eliza felt an immediate connection.

"Where was it? Was it in my dreams?"

As if in a wave of emotion, it donned

"Is it not the Pashtun enchantress who stole her husband's heart; the voluptuous beauty with blue eyes, the heroine in the folklore of Michael alias Kamal."

Letting go off Xariah, Eliza took Zohal's hands in a warm clasp and looked into her eyes in teen adulation. Zohal was never her rival; she was the reason for her adulation of Michael. Her long-lost friend whom she had never met.

"Xariah's Ama, what a pleasant surprise that you would accompany my son and his beloved. I am eternally grateful to you for it."

Eliza raised the clasped hands for a peck on her palms in the warmest of welcome Zohal had received in her life. Those moments stood still for Zohal. She pinched herself to wake her from the dream. It was so surreal and the least she had expected. That moment Zohal felt diminutive, even her great-grandchild was taller than her. She felt cheated by her emotions as she awaited the meeting with Eliza.

Zohal took Eliza in a warm embrace. Now she knew where Salim's warmth and care for everyone came from.

The chip off the old block was his mother.

✹✹✹

Chapter 22

Eliza, Flashback

The cowdung flung by her mother stood straight on her face. Through the drippings that hazed her vision, she saw the most handsome man walk towards her.

She froze inside, her heart still fluttering, enamoured by the sheer presence of Michael alias Kamal, who was calling on the family to see the girl he was going to marry.

The folklore in Perumbavoor, the town famous for its timber, was that Michael, who accompanied his brother, a viceroy's commissioned officer in the army, had converted to marry the Brigadier's daughter, who fell in love with him at first sight.

The girls believed the fable, as they had known what a charmer Michael was. They felt a tinge of pride swelling, knowing even the Pashtun beauty with blue eyes could not resist him.

Giving a gentle and comforting smile to Eliza, Michael proceeded to the house with Eliza's mother speeding ahead, calling out to her husband and gasping, "Michael Ethi; Mole kanaan."

Michael is home to see Eliza.

As Michael disappeared into the precincts, charm gave way to reality, and tears streamed down her dung-splattered cheeks. She wanted to kill her mother. She mentally prepared herself to bear the consequences of a life in jail. The only thing that was holding her back was a possible life with Michael. She decided to wait for a more opportune moment to settle the score with her mother. With Michael by her side, the task would be much easier and less emotionally draining. Maybe he will find a way to help her mother escape the indictment. She thought of numerous possibilities and finally concluded that the best option was to pack her off to Karachi.

Elisa's grandfather, Verghese Mappilai, owned a quarter of the town, having built his fortune as an astute money lender, both revered and despised, showing no mercy to those who defaulted. He had two children, Jacob and Eliza's father, Avira. Jacob was in the mould of his father, same gait, commanding voice, and ready for risk to build his own empire.

The town of Perumbavoor was the link to the misty mountains of Munnar from Kochi, the cosmopolitan city where the backwater lake of Vembanad merged with the Arabian Sea in a romantic embrace. The Marikkar family was the most prominent among merchants in Kochi. They had roots in Persia, coming to Kerala for trade long ago. Zulfikar, the youngest in the family, had an instant love for the land and convinced his father to allow him to stay back and make Travancore his home. Married to the descendant of the first Moslem traders to land at Krangannore, he founded the Marikkar Trading Company.

Marikkars, being astute merchants, stayed committed to the whites. What more could they have done? The ever-pleasing among the royals were more than willing to bare their legs to have their comforts ensured than to raise a finger for their own people.

But the decedents of Zulfikar stood up, doing a generous, though dangerous, act of caring for the needy, parting a good fortune of their wealth that they were entitled to and that they earned by being the whites' trusted interlocutor with the rulers, whom they found disgustingly self-serving.

Closer to the world wars, Marikkar saw an opportunity to be part of a burgeoning business class. Even before the Royalty had it, the Rolls Royce was in his collection. Marikkar started the first bus service in the city. The allure of Cochin with its port and backwaters and Munnar in the western ghats, which spotted the comforting environs of Scottish weather, were the whites' favourite spots in Kerala. The Britisher's love for good tea had Finlay Company set up the largest tea estate in the world. Munnar had a beautifully manicured golf course too, which effectuated its Scottish charm.

The longest of Marikkar's bus services was from Cochin to Munnar. Jacob wanted to learn to drive, the first step to owning a bus and building a fleet later. The easiest way for him was to be the sidekick of the driver. Verghese Mappilai was distraught and angry with his son when he heard of Jacob's choice. He had loftier plans for his son. Jacob would inherit his money-lending business. Verghese had fathomed that his younger son would be a misfit for his business. He was too gentle and genial for it. He wanted to protect Avira's future and went on to buy swaths of land and rice fields for him. He taught him to till land and ride bullock-drawn carriages. He was good at both. His skill at acing the bullocks was unmatched.

Avira had trained them for a *fly-by-wire decent,* as in modern aircrafts, for his late-night returns from the wholesale market at Kothamangalam, half a day away. To keep him company during those returns, he would speak to the crickets, who answered all his queries with their shriek replies, to his great comfort. In winter, it nighted early, and the ride back and the ride back would be all through darkness, the road empty. On those occasions, he would talk simultaneously to his bullock twins, who donned gold-laced horn-gear, along with the crickets. The bullock twins replied in silence, unlike the crickets, but they had all the answers for Avira.

A mile from home was *Iringol Kaavu,* the temple drawn inspiration from scriptures, the famed abode of Maya, goddess Durga herself rising in wrath as Kansa, the demon king, decided to kill a girl despite being foretold she was no threat to him.

It stood as a testimony of faith, splendour, and awe. To Avira, there was an add-on version of the celestial imp who sought tobacco-laced betel leaf chew—to be drawn into her lustful embrace, to be drained of blood, even before a chance to immerse in her. She was Yakshi, more beautiful than an apsara. She lived atop the fat palm 'pana'. Iringol Kaavu had plenty of them.

Avira did not like her.

But he was worried that she would get him if their eyes locked. A furlong from Kaavu, he would have the autopilot on. He would sheath himself in fake slumber to have the cart taxied to its resting place. Listening to the silence of the bell gated by them, he would awaken and have yoke done with his bullock twins, leading to a sumptuous dinner and rest at the cow castle.

Jacob could have done far better, riding his own fleet of buses, but he erred. Avira rued that his brother never attempted to understand his father. So talented he was, what was the need for him to turn a vagabond rather than join his father in taking over the mantle of the business? Avira tried his best in his spoken silence, but Jacob never relented.

It's said your worst enemy is reborn as your son to atone for the deeds of previous lives. Maybe Jacob was that to his father. He felt helpless but was firm about carrying forward the legacy of the Chamakalayil family if that was the will of his father.

For Varghese Mappilai, the ignominy was unbearable. He felt deceived by his son; it was unpardonable. He was determined to leave a lasting lesson for his act that lowered the standing of the family. Despite the best of efforts by Avira, even offering to bequeath half his inheritance to his brother, his father was firm on his decision. He feared that Jacob's foolishness would hurt his younger son and family.

In a week, he had his will made, bequeathing half his wealth to Jacob's children and not leaving a penny for his son.

Jacob died a pauper.

✸✸✸

Chapter 23

Michael, the Rising Star

Michael was the rising student leader in Travancore for the Congress party that was spearheading the freedom movement.

He had joined the Quit India Movement while still in school. Leading the student march, he was arrested twice and jailed. Being a juvenile, he was let go earlier. It's in the cramped jail cell that he made lasting friendships with men who gave selflessly to the movement, some of them going on to serve with elan in the government of independent India.

People had started celebrating even before the midnight of freedom. The half-naked fakir, as Gandhi was called by the British, had mesmerised a whole nation with his quit India call through the path of ahimsa and non-violence.

The freedom fighters fought hard, but no blood was spilled; the British spilled a lot of it, kicking, beating, and shooting at peaceful protestors. Legions of them were struck down by police, only for the ones lining behind them to rise to take their place. The beatings stopped only when the aggressor's hands dropped in pain.

Gandhi was a visionary who could see the future. In free India, he wanted an equitable society that built villages. He had concluded that the present leadership of the party would yoke the freedom movement for an easy ride to power. He called for disbanding the Indian National Congress through a resolution at the AICC, the core body of the party, which read, *'It resolves to disband the existing Congress organisation and flower into a society to serve the people."*

Acharya Kripalani, the AICC President who saw the country to independence, was the first to resign.

So did Michael.

The Praja Socialist Party, PSP, meaning "People's Fabian Congregation" was born thus, with the theme progressive but anti-capitalist. Acharya and his followers did not want the Congress Party to usher in viceroyal rule in the garb of national fervour. Many were wary of it.

In the following election, PSP won many states; the government at the centre was formed by Congress under Nehru.

The state of Kerala was formed almost a decade later based on linguistic reorganization. Till then, it was the erstwhile princely state of Travancore, with Pattom Thanu Pillai, fondly called Pattom, as its prime minister. It was a PSP government. Meanwhile, Michael, who was majoring in English, caught the PM's attention as an upcoming young leader. He was fond of him.

Pothanicad village, near Michael's home, did not have a school. Children had to tread well, and it was gaining momentum as a popular movement. Michael knew something had to be done, and he had a scheme. Michael was one of the few who had entry right up to Pattom's bedroom. Sneaking in the next day, Michael brewed Pattom's favourite coffee, laced with pepper and cinnamon, and surprised him with it as he returned from his morning stroll.

The people of Pothanicad carried Michael on their shoulders as he waved government approval to the delight of the whole village. Destiny had Michael as its first headmaster before he turned twenty-four.

Kerala had become one under the reorganisation of Indian states. Its people were ecstatic. The name Kerala was unique. It signified its romance with the coconut tree, which formed an intimate relationship with its people. From curries to thatches, Kera, or coconut, was part of their lives. Stretching across Travancore and Malabar, her people spoke the same language in fifty different dialects that needed a translator at times.

Fable had its enchanting beauty owed to Hindu mythology; the creator, Lord Vishnu, in his avatar Parasuram, wanted an abode for himself. Throwing his axe to the southern seas, he created a land mass as slim as the most beautiful apsara, with the western ghats as its bosom and fresh water lakes as its navel, with an array of rivers to feed her nectar from the mountains. From the shore to the hills, a mere forty miles away, the heaving mountains caressed down the clouds to wet the land throughout the year. How could the spices not bloom in this land?

Acharya Kripalani, the supremo of the PSP party, was to visit soon to galvanise the party for the election. Pattom had to ensure that Kripalani's visit went well. One of his key concerns was that people would not understand his language, English or Hindi. His message would be lost if he did not have the right transcriber.

Pattom had someone in mind.

The state car entered the men's hostel and inquired for Michael. As he was ushered into the Chief Minister's office (the *PM had become CM of the reorganised state by then*), Pattom lost no time in briefing the young man. The towering Pattom looked at Michael with gladdened pride.

"Michael, you know of Acharya's arrival the following week. Collect the schedule from the Chief Secretary." Pattom paused, and Michael nodded but had no clue what to do next.

"You are assigned the personal secretary to the chairman during the visit, with all resources as needed at your disposal."

He dismissed the boy with a 'you may go now' gesture. The enormity of it was just sinking in. As he turned to walk, the Chief Minister got up from the chair and walked to Michael. Patting the young man in appreciation, he said, "By the way, Michael, you did a brilliant job at Gandhi Park. Keep it up!"

Michael remembered the occasion. Ashok Mehta, General Secretary of PSP, was delivering his address at Gandhi Park. Being an economist, his oratory was laced with economic policies that the party would follow and the concepts behind them. The transcriber's performance was so dismal that the crowd got restive.

The Chief Minister sharing the podium was worried, and that's when he felt a soft nudge on his shoulder, Michael, *"Sir, let me do it."*

The rest was history. Ashok Mehta got a standing ovation, the only one he had received since he left his alma mater. Little did he realise that the applause was for Michael, who narrated the story as his own, far better than Mehta spoke.

Acharya had a whirlwind tour of the state, and he was extremely happy with the outcome. He had gotten fond of the boy too, who had coordinated it meticulously. Michael had an uncanny take on the politics of the state, which was vastly different from the rest of the nation. South India had not witnessed the carnage of partition. Hindus and Muslims lived in peace here and wondered how the carnage post-independence could take place. The brothers, who fought alongside each other for freedom, were butchering each other when they got it.

"A million people's breath was snuffed away as they waited to inhale the air of freedom."

Was freedom worth it? he wondered.

From whom was the freedom? A human sacrifice that colossal could have gotten India its freedom two centuries ago; hate and mistrust endured between Hindus and Muslims.

In the state of Kerala, the religious makeup was in stark contrast to the rest of India, where the Hindu population was 85 percent. In Kerala, it was just over half; the balance split between Christians and Muslims was almost equal. The regional spread too had its queerness and needed a different poll strategy altogether. Michael had defining knowledge of the interplay, and it surprised Acharya how the young mind had gathered the wisdom of a veteran.

As they reached Cochin, from where he would take the flight to Delhi the next day, Acharya called in Michael for a personal brief. Even the Chief Minister, who was present, was not privy to what transpired.

"Michael, you need to shift base to Delhi. The state canvas is too small for you. I need you with me in Delhi."

Michael couldn't believe his ears. He was elated at the appreciation of the chairman.

"I will make all the arrangements. My office will send you tickets for travel the following week or whenever you are ready. Young man, you have done me proud."

The state car dropped Michael off at home. He was seeing Eliza and Devon after a month, and both could not contain the joy of seeing him. Devon ran to his father and did not leave him till he fell deep asleep in his arms. Eliza too had slumbered on Michael's shoulder, cuddling him tighter than Devon, so as to never let him go.

Michael felt so fortunate.

Acharya's words rescinded as he slipped in to sleep, holding his precious family in a warm cuddle.

Eliza and Devon joined Michael as he went to see Acharya. Devon was thrilled to jump into the front seat of the car that came to take them. Eliza was so proud of her husband as the neighbourhood descended to see Michael's new car. Few said it was the Chief Minister's gift to Michael.

"If you could get us a school, is the car bigger?

Eliza clutched Michael's arm in a show of *'he's mine and mine only'* to the envy of the young girls around.

Acharya was very happy to see Michael's family.

"You should have given me an inkling, Michael; I would have gotten a gift for your son".

He took Eliza by both her hands, patted her lovingly on the cheeks, and said,

"You are lucky to have a husband so brilliant." She blushed.

Turning to Michael, he said, "I think you are luckier to have a girl like Eliza who epitomises your land of rare beauty."

Eliza did not understand a word of what was told about her, but she knew it was good of her. Eliza and Devon, with a mound of sweets gifted by Acharya, left for their home.

Michael accompanied the chairman to the airport. As he finished his check-in, Michael requested a moment with Acharya. With deep intent, he listened to Michael's words.

"The time spent with you is the most memorable in my life, and it has taught me what it would have taken me a decade to learn. Your invite to Delhi to be a part of your team is a once-in-a-lifetime opportunity that only one in a million gets. I am so thankful to you for it." As Michael paused, Acharya gave him time to compose his emotions.

"My wife and son were so happy to see you. It's only when they are mature enough will they realise the enormity of this meeting. *Acharya, I cannot leave my young wife and son and join you in Delhi.* Forgive me. I will do all that's needed for the party in Travancore to my last breath."

Acharya was moved. He knew Michael was making a political blunder, but he could not force him anymore. Acharya took Michael in a deep embrace and held him there for a long time. As they parted, Acharya said, "Michael, you have made the right decision. Heart-over-head leaders are what we need."

Acharya blessed Michael in the true Indian custom of placing his hand over his head, eyes closing in silent prayer.

Tears welled in Michael, tears of pride.

The next election to the state assembly was a watershed moment. Michael was the candidate from the Perumbavoor constituency, which had a considerable presence of the communist cadre. The main contenders were the Congress, which had won the constituency continuously since the first election, and the Communist Party of India, with its roots deeply entrenched in the social fabric of Kerala, with its veteran leader, EMS, a former Congress stalwart, leading it. The communists were eyeing a revival in Kerala to clinch the constituency that would give them a foothold in central Travancore, one that had evaded them for long.

The leadership of the Communist Party sent a senior comrade to meet Michael with an important message in the run-up to the election: unequivocal support, with the condition that he should fight the election as an independent.

He elucidated the reason too.

"Michael, you know the PSP and the Communist Party of India are not in an electoral alliance here or, for that matter, anywhere in India. We have complimenting ideologies, but without an alliance, we can never have you supported, even if it meant we lost the election."

He continued, "Be with us; a young leader of your stature and calibre will be an asset to state politics. More importantly, a boon to your home constituency."

Michael was moved.

He had no words to express his gratitude for the faith in him and his people. It was true that their ideologies were far closer to each other than any other political party, and a common fight against Congress was the need of the hour to bring in what the father of the nation had desired when he asked the Congress party to be disbanded.

Moving across to where the senior comrade was seated, he took his hands in gratitude and said, "Comrade, I never expected this honour—the faith that your party has placed in me and you coming personally to convey it—a rare gift."

Stopping for a moment, he continued, "As you know, sir, I have built my party from scratch here. Half my income goes to maintaining its office. The foothold to challenge Congress by ourselves will take time, but it will happen one day. What you have offered me is a winning formula, for sure. A fool alone will reject it."

Michael closed his eyes to compose himself for the big moment.

"*I am that fool, for I cannot abandon my baby PSP*. I joined the party on the day of its formation, heeding a call. Had I remained with Congress, I would have been its candidate today. This could be the biggest blunder in my political career, killing my parliamentary foray." He paused again. "I choose it with all humility. Till it survives, PSP will be my party."

The comrade could not believe his ears. He was sad that he would have to work against

Michael. But the young man had won his heart for life.

In the ensuing election, the Communist Party supported independent from the constituency, and they formed the government. Michael had to sell his ancestral inheritance to pay for the expenses of the election, which had sparse party funding.

Eliza was sad for her husband but proud of his decision. Avira could never forgive his son-in-law. He would say, "What a fool! Let it not be for him. But for the young who trusted and supported him with their hearts, didn't he owe it to them? *A blank check to victory uncashed!*"

PSP did not survive long.

With the resurgence of Congress under Indira Gandhi, daughter of the first prime minister, PSP saw dust. The original party of Acharya and Pattom faded into oblivion.

So did Michael.

The teacher in him bloomed from then on. Michael was invited to be part of the largest high school coming up in Malabar under the Catholic Church. The founding fathers of the school, Fr. Varkey and Michael, hit off the moment they met at the bishop's house.

Michael's life changed forever.

From the suave Karachi teen to the rising star of the prominent political party to a village teacher, it had turned a full circle. Pin-striped suit to barefoot soldier, the elan stayed.

Did he regret his choices? The reporter covering his story asked, "Would you rewind the clock if there was a way and take the path to political glory now?"

Michael was lucid in his answer.

"Yes, my friend, for sure. *But my choices would be the same.*"

He was a rare breed.

***

Chapter 24

Till Death Do Us All Part

Zohal came to know of Michael's death from Salim. She cried.

At that moment, her heart went out to Eliza, his partner and wife for decades. She wanted to be with Eliza now. Without waiting for Salim, Zohal boarded the next flight to India.

The house that was Eliza's ancestral home, where she was born, was brimming with people, paying their last respects to someone the whole land loved and adored. She asked for Eliza on arrival. She was in her room, with people trickling in to convey their condolences. Eliza thanked each for their kindness and their love for Michael, which brought them there.

By her side were Ariyan and his wife, Jaanu, as if a constant tail. Zohal saw none of their children other than Ayesha with her, and she felt sad. As Zohal was ushered in, Eliza gestured for all but her daughter to leave. She held Zohal close to her and kissed her cheek. Zohal could hardly contain her tears and sobs.

Eliza did not cry.

She had a mystical calm on her face, and Zohal was unable to fathom the depth of it. She wore it with elegance.

Both of them went together to the side of Michael. Seating her beside Ayesha, she excused herself. "Zohal, I need to personally thank all those coming to pay their last respect. Many have come a long way, and the least I should do is greet them."

Zohal patted her in approval. She was proud of the way Eliza was handling the moment.

Michael looked frail in the confines of the coffin.

Yet his face had not lost its naughty glimmer.

She sighed.

The town saw the biggest farewell of its time. The proud son of theirs, who romanticised a whole generation, taught the young to dream, and was there when they wanted him, was on his last journey.

The sky too darkened, with a strong drizzle, nature showering its petals of cool dew on him.

"You come from the earth; you go back to it."

The bishop concluded his words as the sheath of cover was drawn over his face, consuming him to eternity. Nobody cried except his daughter, Ayesha. All wanted to give him a farewell laced with a smile, one that Michael always carried. Zohal felt it was a fitting farewell to the man she so deeply loved.

As the hustle died down, Eliza asked Zohal to be by her side as she met her children later that evening. Eliza was tired; she closed her eyes and lay on her bed, resting for a while. After a warm shower and a cup of coffee with Zohal and Ayesha, Eliza asked all to be assembled in the family chamber. It was in the chamber that all important announcements were made.

Dressed in a cashmere silk sari with exquisitely handcrafted Mandala flowers, she strode slowly but firmly to the chamber. Zohal remembered that it was Xariah's gift to Eliza when they visited first. She looked elegant and beautiful in it.

With Ayesha at her side, she began, with a loving glance at all her children. The air was thick; this was the first time they had seen their mother so elegantly attired, extremely composed, and speaking with absolute authority.

It scared a few.

"I am fortunate to have you as my children. My husband and I have raised you to the best of our capabilities through triumphs and tribulations." She paused.

"I have had very significant differences with your father on intimate and delicate matters known to both of us. There was a time when I felt deeply cheated. I thought our marriage would end. During those turbulent times, it was Appachan, my father, who held me close and asked me to see reason beyond the precincts of infidelity. He reminded me that I was the fulcrum of the family, including his. Your father too sensed the gravity of the situation, and since then, we have lived a life understanding each other's perspective."

As she paused to sip water, the eerie silence gave way to bewilderment as well as a deep appreciation for the candour. You could feel a tinge of tears in the eyes of a few.

Eliza continued, "My children, I have prepared the will."

This was the moment all anxiously looked forward to and feared too.

Eliza continued, "This is the house I was born in—what my grandfather built for us. This is being converted into a museum of art in memory of my father."

There was a huge murmur and voices of disapproval. Eliza continued,

'My eldest son, who stays here now, will have full access to the living facilities of the estate as his own and will oversee the gallery till his time. I hope to see his plays that I missed as a young mother. The legal formalities for the same have been completed."

Turning to her advocate, Ajay, she asked that it be shared with all. She paused for a moment in thought, her emotions flashing by, and she continued.

"The family chamber will now be known in the name of my sister Sarah, the one I could not protect."

For the first time, Zohal saw the frail side of Eliza, tears were rolling down her cheek. Composing herself, she continued,

"The only picture I have of her is the one pinned to my heart—my chirpy butterfly." Besides, there would be an endowment that would go to support a girl child every year until she completes her college education. You know the way I supported Lolita. The expense for the same too has been factored in. The savings of my husband, which you know are quite substantial, will go towards it."

That was the last straw. A few wanted to cry.

As she concluded, Eliza said, "As far as I am concerned, I have my husband's pension to live on and the room that I use now. Your mother is in good health, and she will manage."

Thanking everyone, she rose to retire to the confines of her room. The heaviness lifted, and her heart fluttered like a butterfly, in all hues.

Epilogue

Zohal led Eliza, eyes closed.

A few steps more, and then a flat surface walk.

Zohal turned Eliza a few times, like the spinning wheel, till she lost all sense of direction.

Eliza could feel the cool breeze caressing her; it had a soothing fragrance too, she realised. And Zohal let go of her hand covering Eliza's eyes.

"Let it open like a morning flower, at its sanguine pace, imbibing the nature around." She said softly to Eliza.

Eliza could not believe her eyes. She looked in heart-pounding awe at the beauty of the Himalayas unfolding before her.

"Is this paradise?"

Zohal's ancestral home had a joint owner now. Eliza!

About the Author

Sanjeev Panackal Thomas did his schooling at Lawerence School, Lovedale, India, and completed his engineering and Masters in Business Studies. He had a successful corporate career spanning Europe, America, and India before becoming an entrepreneur. His passion for writing has taken him through this novel which has glimpses of his own life and stories foretold to him by his ancestors, encompassing a tale spanning three generations.

A birthday gift to my wife, Annie

Dated July 5, 2023

Manufactured by Amazon.ca
Bolton, ON